LAST NIGHT AT THE BRAIN THIEVES BALL

LAST NIGHT AT THE BRAIN THIEVES BALL

a novel by
Scott Spencer

Houghton Mifflin Company Boston
1973

PS
3569
P455
L3

12/1973
Genl

FIRST PRINTING C

Printed in the United States of America

Library of Congress Cataloging in Publication Data

Spencer, Scott.
    Last night at the brain thieves ball.

    I. Title.
PZ4.S7465Las   PS3569.P455   813'.5'4   73-4805
ISBN 0-395-17125-3

To Devorah, Kid Zeit,
and Eleven One Three Three One

O miserable minds of men! O blind hearts! In what darkness of life, in what great dangers ye spend this little span of years!

LUCRETIUS

LAST NIGHT AT THE BRAIN THIEVES BALL

1

MY DESK IS SHAPED like a kidney and has a slight wobble. I have finally learned to draw the curtains to the small window in the parallelogram of senseless noise they call my office. That's something: what we call progress. Before me are five lime green folders (I can see the strips of lamplight on their shiny surfaces) filled with photostats, carbon copies, photographs, test scores, intercepted letters, witty memos, dream summaries, fingerprints, thumbnail sketches, EEG charts, oscillograph readings, EMG abstracts, GSR readings, EKG charts — a whole hulking beast of immoral information that pirouettes painfully around the one indisputable fact: I am a brain thief.

I am a brain thief and I wish to repent. You can quote me. Facts galore! It is getting me down, this business of brain thievery, this morning coffee in a Styrofoam cup. All day I am assaulted by a stereophonic barrage of hostile noise. Upstairs, the Force Recruiters are learning to kick down doors. At this very instant I hear the One, Two,

Three . . . KICK of Miss Mitchell's Force Recruiters above, followed by the clatter of fifty doors onto the heavily varnished gymnasium floor. They clatter floorward, the dummy doors, at precisely the same instant. Miss Mitchell is very strict about that. And anyone she trains as a Force Recruiter had better toe that line. I can't be sure, of course, but that's, I am told, how things are up in the gym — all those huge fierce men and Miss Mitchell, in her mouse gray jumpsuit with an enormous silver whistle dangling from her neck. "All the doors must fall at the same instant," she probably says, and looks at the Force Recruiters apocalyptically.

Aside from that, I have been hearing footsteps that seem to slow down as they pass my office, speed up and vanish.

And then, I am having one of those days when even my simplest thoughts echo sententiously in the vast cellular silence of my brain, reverberating endlessly through gray corridors.

I have seen Miss Mitchell, our Violence Coordinator, in the cafeteria and think she's a real piece. It is one of my dreams to sneak into the gymnasium and watch her train the Force Recruiters. But it is not allowed. Visiting. Or fraternization. Or much of anything. It's a tight ship. Everywhere you look there's a shoulder to the wheel, an eye on the ball.

◆　◆　◆

It's the leg closest to my left foot. Even the slight pressure I use to write these words causes my desk to wobble. Whoever is in charge of such things must consider my

2

interior decorations a matter of complete indifference. I have written repeatedly that I am in need of a new desk and the request has not been acknowledged.

The five lime green folders are still before me. A faint odor of Xerox wafts from them. Miss Dorfman, the secretary assigned to me, is in Arizona on her vacation, visiting her insane cousin, of whom I have heard far far too much. The last time my desk began to wobble she fixed it. But I can't remember for the life of me what it was she did. With her hands. Her strong, salmon-colored hands. "There, Mr. Galambos," she said to me, sitting on the floor and grinning, "fixed!"

Before me, right next to the green folders, is an orange and magenta sign that Mr. Worthington "suggests" we hang in some suitable place. IMAGINATION: THE BIG PLUS. Although there may exist men in this organization who are more powerful and important than Mr. Worthington, I do not have contact with them. Mr. W. is my boss and every once in a while he comes into my cubicle and asks me how it's going. He is an old, bland gent for whom I have a strange, practically slavish adoration. Yesterday, around ten in the morning, he came in and asked me, "How's it going, Paul?" and offered me a mint. Then to my surprise and, yes, gratification he complimented me on my work on the gamma motor neuron. Not that I am unaccustomed to being complimented — my work here is far above the competence level — but I was faintly uncertain about my gamma motor neuron hypotheses. Through a clever manipulation of some stray data on Subject #3-R-d (a Roberta Merkin of Grand Rapids, Michigan), I was able to postulate that changes in furni-

3

ture styles cause changes in posture which cause changes in susceptibility to anxiety stimuli. In other words, it is possible to design breakfast nook chairs that will send legions of men to work each day with their teeth absolutely on edge, their knuckles white. Of course, for the office we will suggest chairs that will counteract the nasty neuronal nag and put everyone quite at ease. Thus the gamma neuron will shift dramatically man's loyalty to his work place, a task no number of company picnics and stock option plans could possibly accomplish . . .

♦ ♦ ♦

Perhaps I am one of the most brilliant, lonely men alive. My brilliance and loneliness seem to have no boundaries. I have been working for New England Sensory Testing, Engineering, and Research (NESTER) for four months now and I'm beginning to feel it was all a terrible mistake, a huge error which every passing day compounds.

Once I was an associate professor of experimental psychology at a university on the eastern seaboard of America, and I was having the usual associate professor's luck. My bride, Lydia, had gone back to her family in Forest Hills, New York, with our son, an adopted eight-year-old to whom I was just becoming accustomed. I had alienated permanently the head of my department with a few needless remarks at two o'clock in the morning while wishing him good-bye on his stagelike porch beneath an orange light bulb hideously orbited by a thousand strange insects. Then add the subsequent affair with a nineteen-year-old student who responded to my moist, overripened affections with a nervous breakdown and

4

dropped out of school — to be whisked witlessly back to Newport News by her drunken father and a sassy chauffeur. My tears, real tears, of no interest to history or to anyone, are mentioned here in passing.

When one finds oneself enmeshed in the cold, buzzing logic of a place like NESTER one naturally asks: How did I get here? It's hard to choose a place in time and say: *This* is where it all began. Every day we pass innumerable forks in the road and retracing our steps is usually impossible. But there was a point, say two years ago, call it the Christmas holidays, when my life took on a pointlessness and a tedium that edged me toward the very limits of panic. I could no longer tolerate reading my old, half-good lectures to those smiling semicircles of crosslegged undergraduates. My marriage was as rewarding and invigorating as a few hours in front of a slot machine. I had never in my life been blessed with the gift of popularity but my relations with friends and acquaintances were at an all-time low. The fellow whom I had casually — perhaps too casually — considered my best friend, and who lived a scant 250 miles from me, failed to inform me when his wife gave birth to their daughter, for instance. My finances were neither in shambles nor in a state of growth. The money I made and the money I spent and saved remained constant, and it was clear that this was to be my standard of living for the rest of my days.

I was acutely aware of growing older. I was morbidly conscious of living in a changing world. In an age of upheaval, I wanted to do some upheaving of my own. I was no stranger to the current advances in science, warfare, sex, and men's fashions. I would read about them

5

in the magazines and see them on television. Speeches, threats, proclamations, confessions. But none of them included me. I wasn't a part of the times. I wasn't noticed and, were I to disappear, I wouldn't be missed. I joined book clubs. I wrote provocative letters to my senators and congressmen, hoping that I would be one of those blessed academics who is invited to manage the political affairs of a dynamic candidate solely on the basis of a well-phrased letter. I subscribed to over fifty magazines. I adopted bizarre opinions. I followed everything that was current with a sharp, critical eye, waiting for history to rub off on me. But of course it never would.

Even my work in the laboratory was beginning to pale. The lab had long been my refuge, but how many times can you watch a bunch of pink-eyed rats nose their way around a sheet-metal maze and still think it's interesting? Even the little embellishments, like electric shocks and ringing bells that would send the hapless rodents into a defecating tizzy, added nothing to my interest in these routine exercises. And it wasn't only the routine exercises that bored me. The whole thing bored me. Even my rather neat contribution to the scientific understanding of DNA left me cold. After all, I asked myself, what did it matter? It didn't serve to connect me to anything. My world was still a small and essentially a shabby one. I took to thinking of my colleagues as a bunch of squares. I began to fantasize about life on an expense account, my name in gossip columns. I brooded over the fact that I wasn't an atomic physicist. If I were an atomic physicist, foreign governments would try to tempt me to defect. I might be involved in tumultuous controversy. Mayhem!

But no. That wasn't in the cards for me. I wasn't getting anywhere. I grew sideburns and bought a pair of two-toned shoes.

Then I came across NESTER's two-sentence classified ad in a weekly magazine of refined opinion. "Dynamic Progressive Company Seeks Psychologists for Public Relations Program/ Full Experimental and Executive Freedom/ Unlimited Opportunity." I had always been a habitual reader of employment advertising — I pored over the classifieds like a quadraplegic over sporting goods catalogues, with that same futile enthusiasm, that same discerning desperation. My sense of futility found its roots not in my personality but in my history. I had, that is to say, answered scores of notices and never once came even close to landing a job that I wanted. Either my applications went unacknowledged or I was urged to meet with some raving mediocrity who wanted to entice me to take a position either similar to or shabbier than my own. But there was something about NESTER's notice that excited all that was juvenile and optimistic in me.

I stayed up late into the night, writing them a long letter — though I didn't at that time know to whom I was writing. It was strictly a matter of "Dear Sirs" and a post office box. I described my qualifications, expressed my willingness to change jobs, to sell my house, and change towns, and said I looked forward to hearing from them.

◆ ◆ ◆

Two weeks after unknowingly nibbling NESTER's bait, I became aware of two muscular men with short yellow hair following me about the campus. When I first noticed them I guessed they were recent enrollees, back from Southeast Asia and finishing up their education on the GI Bill. They had that cruel, experienced look of Vietnam veterans. It was the beginning of the winter semester and they both signed up for my class in Classical Conditioning. I took note of their calm, vaguely malevolent eyes as soon as I walked into the small room where I pontificated. My first assumption was that they were out to give me a hard time because I had signed a number of petitions and proclamations denouncing the war and had a few months before spent a couple of hours with an assortment of academicians and liberal townsfolk in a silent vigil in front of the post office, the only federal building in the area. They were registered under the names Clinton Factor and Ray Pernod, names which, for some reason, sent little chunks of ice tumbling through my circulatory system. I had meant to check up on them in the administration building but, characteristically, I never got around to it. All my years I had been plagued with a life-style in which the most insignificant details of my days obstructed my ability to cope with the larger forces governing me. In other words, a mild desire to listen to a Mozart concert on FM radio would send me racing home after my final lecture instead of going to the administration building as I should have.

Not that checking up on them would have done any good. Undoubtedly, their records would have been neatly filed and in order and I would have looked at them, nodded, put them back, and returned to my life with a sense of security as false as my wife Lydia's smile, if I can be permitted a bit of gratuitous bitterness.

It is not altogether uncommon for associate professors to be manhandled or even slain by irate students, but such outbursts usually occur after final examinations and grades. So even though I was aware that Factor and Pernod were in my field of vision (and I in theirs) with an eerie frequency, I didn't worry about it too much. Once, when I noticed them nursing bottles of Heineken near my table at the Gooch (a local hangout where I occasionally convinced young women to share meals with me), I approached them with an open smile and we all shook hands. "How do you like school?" I asked them. They glanced back and forth at each other, apparently unsure to whom the question had been directed. I looked at Clinton Factor, who was the slightly smaller of the two and whose squared chin was a mass of small white scars. He said, "We like it fine, sir," and Pernod called the waitress over and asked for their check. "And how do you like it, sir?" asked Pernod, smiling at me. He glanced at the check, handed it to Factor, and slapped a quarter and a dime onto the powder blue Formica table.

A week later someone pushed me down the stairs as I was on my way to lunch. I was on the third-floor landing of the social science building, holding a notebook and a lunch bag. I felt a pair of strong hands smash into the small of my back and I screamed, and then the stairs leaped up to my face and there was darkness. There was not, unfortunately, a loss of consciousness. I was acutely aware of my body striking the hard wooden surfaces, my ankles dragging, my muscles twisting, my elbows banging, my head splitting. I sat up when I reached the bottom still holding on to my lunch bag, though my notebook and papers had been scattered. A few flickering gray shafts of vision pierced the fearsome blackness that had descended upon me with my fall. Then I saw perhaps a dozen horrified students lurching in my direction and behind them one of my big blond nemeses — Factor or Pernod, I did not know which — fading down the hall.

The next thing I knew I was in an ambulance. I came to briefly and saw a white-jacketed attendant withdraw a hypo from my arm, and then I felt my tongue swell in my mouth and I was gone again. I awoke in the university hospital, in a private room. Denny Grinnel, the young chairman of the psychology department and by now no friend of mine, was at my bedside with his young son Farley, who in my confusion I first took to be my own adopted boy, Andrew. "Hello there," Denny said when my eyes opened.

"Hello," I said.

"What in the hell happened to you?" he asked.

"Someone pushed me down the stairs," I answered, not aware of any particular pain.

"Hmmm?" he said, moving closer to me and putting his lanky arm around his son's shoulders.

"I said some dirty son of a bitch shoved me down the goddamn stairs."

He shook his head. "All right. Don't strain yourself. We'll talk later." He stood up. I realized my voice, clear enough to me, was no more than an assortment of sub-human mumbles to Denny. "You just rest. You've had a nasty spill."

"I was pushed."

"Hmmmm? What? Oh, never mind. Dr. Pitch is looking after you. A good man. He told me you've broken no bones and it looks like you'll be out of here real soon. You go in for x rays in an hour or so — "

"Why don't you let me do the explaining?" a voice interrupted. It was Dr. Pitch, who entered rubbing his enormous red hands together and —

♦ ♦ ♦

One of Mr. Worthington's numerous lackeys rapped on my door just a few minutes ago. I snapped closed this notebook and jumped up, practically toppling my trembling desk. (A flash of fluorescence reflected over its surface as it swayed.) "Who is it?" I croaked.

The door opened and it was Tom Simon, Mr. W.'s private secretary or liaison officer or valet — who knows what he was? "Note from the Man Upstairs," he said, shaking a long, lime green envelope at me. I took it from him and he turned on his heel and left.

I ripped open the svelte envelope, tearing part of its contents. I have always been overcome with greed and expectation when opening mail. Inside, there was a sheet of pale yellow paper, folded once down the center. On it, written with a green felt-tipped pen, were "Keep up the good work" and Mr. Worthington's full, rich signature — each letter in his name looked like an animate object. I sat down heavily in my meager swivel chair and turned until I faced my narrow window. Outside, on the compound's manicured grounds, spring was beginning. The lawn was piebald. Right now, the sun is going down somewhere behind me and night moves across the lawn like an enormous shadow, turning the grass deep purple and the blotches of snow steel gray.

Keep up the good work? What is that supposed to mean? Normally, I would take it as a routine compliment for my work here — for I *am* quite good at what I do — but coming as it did when I was in the midst of writing my confession and exposé it seems like a warning. It's as if Mr. W. is quite aware of what I am up to in here and has let me know in his own inimitable, subtle fashion. When you are surrounded by brain thieves — indeed when you are a brain thief yourself — you cannot expect to have very many secrets. The game begins!

♦ ♦ ♦

As I was saying (days have passed), Dr. Pitch entered my hospital room, rubbing his enormous, meaty hands together and sniffling. He gave me a cursory look-over, not even touching me. "Nothing is wrong with you," he said, smiling. "You are only taking space in a crowded hospital. I will have to falsify your forms or they will just kick you right the hell out of here." He glanced at his watch. "Good Lord," he exclaimed, "it's almost eight o'clock." And then he left. Denny and Denny's son left on his heels. I was alone.

Two days passed and I was visited by no one. One of the better reasons for making friends is to insure that certain people will feel obliged to visit you in the hospital. My only solace was that I had a private room and didn't have to endure the endless stream of concerned pals, children, lovers, fans, and apostles of some roommate with a bone spur. I was in a funk. All of my tests were negative and after they were run I received little attention from the staff. No one took my temperature or gave me sponge baths. I made a pest of myself. I spilled my lunch and demanded that another tray be brought to me. I said scandalous things in the hope that I might incite someone to stay and rebut me. I felt like the most insignificant person on earth. Finally, I called Lydia at her mother's apartment in Forest Hills. Lydia's mother's apartment in Forest Hills is called the Grover Cleveland, something that has always amused me. I told her I was in the hospital and she told me she'd been informed. When I learned she already knew I was there, I couldn't bring myself to ask her to come and visit me. I asked her a series of questions pertaining to her well-being — she gave me curt, one-word answers to each — and then I asked to speak to Andrew. He was at the aquarium with Lydia's mother. Good-bye, Lydia. Bye, Paul. Byyyyyeeee.

Late that night, two men crept into my room, taped my mouth closed, bound my hands, put me on a stretcher, and wheeled me away. I had been given a ferocious sleeping pill that evening and my senses were watery and limp. I made an attempt to ask the two men what they were doing but even the most casual physical act seemed unbearably difficult. I wondered casually if I were to be operated on. I couldn't quite remember why I was in the hospital in the first place. I closed my eyes. I was aware of being rolled down a ramp. I heard a door open, felt a rush of sweet cold air, and heard a garbled voice say, "He's waking up." The voice was answered by another as cold, hard, and efficient as an industrial diamond: "So what?" Hearing that, I decided to get up. I made an attempt to throw off the covers and prop myself up on my liquid elbows. I don't know how far I got, because as soon as I stirred something blunt and nasty struck me on the head and I tumbled into darkness like a picture postcard dropped from the thirty-fifth floor down one of those glassed-in mail shutes they build near the elevators in some buildings —

◆　◆　◆

These interruptions are unavoidable. This journal is not the leisurely recollections of a man spending his twilight years in a stone cottage near a pond with nothing to distract him from concentrating on the subtleties of his autobiography save the humorous complaints of his long-serving cottage cleaner. Books and memoirs, I have always thought, are best composed in such stone cottages, or at the Plaza Hotel in New York, or in a small room in Paris with a skylight, or on Cape Cod. This is no place to write. The possibility that this journal might be discovered terrifies me and even when I am writing in it, sometimes, I am barely paying attention. My hand moves across the page while my eyes scan the room — I would not be surprised, I should say, if one of the walls were to slide open and release a claque of frothing Force Recruiters who would bind me in baling wire and drag me through the halls.

But back to my story. I awakened the morning after I'd been spirited from my hospital room and found myself in a rather spacious motel room, which, I was later to learn, was in a Holiday Inn. I felt perfectly fine, except for where I'd been struck. Morning light drifted through the half-opened Venetian blinds in perfect buttery slats. I sat up in bed and faced a stranger. He was about forty-five years old. His features were small and smooth and he couldn't have weighed more than 130 pounds. He had a placid, round face and his feet were no bigger than paperback books. He lit a cigarette — the first of many — inhaled deeply, stared at the tip of the cigarette for a moment, and then smiled at me. "I am so terribly sorry," he said. His voice was soft and textured.

"Where am I?" I asked, not very originally.

"Both Factor and Pernod are newish with us, I'm afraid," he continued, "and they performed their duties with extreme sloppiness."

"Factor? Pernod?" I'm not really sure *what* I said here, but it was something slight and confused. "But?" for instance.

"I would like to fire them," the small gentleman said, "but in terms of the work they do for us they are, really, rather less wicked than most of our new recruits. Perhaps the fault wasn't solely theirs. Poor supervision. I hold myself responsible, if you must know. I wasn't giving the matter its proper attention. I was dividing my time between you and a man in New Haven, who turned out to be, by the way, absolutely unsuitable for us anyhow."

I started to climb out of bed. Surprisingly, I was naked, which slowed me a little. I hadn't any real idea where or with whom I was. My only thought was to remain calm and escape.

"Where are you going?" he asked.

"Umm — I — thought I'd take a look outside . . ."

"Please. Sit down," he said in a way that offered no choice. "My name is Ira Robinson," he said, as soon as I was seated. I pulled a pillow over to cover my naked-

15

ness. "At least, that is the name you shall know me by."
His small, ivory hand darted into his jacket — I expected him to produce a revolver — and he pulled out an envelope. He handed it to me.

It was my application to NESTER, received some two weeks before. "Dear Sirs," it read, "I am writing in response to your advertisement . . ."

For some reason, it all made perfect sense from there. And instead of filling me with anger or fear (common stimuli response for me), the letter filled me with a hush of true admiration. I knew I was dealing with big leaguers. That they, on the basis of a letter, had engineered something as elaborate as my hospitalization and abduction thrilled me beyond words.

"We have considered your application," Ira Robinson said.

"You have?"

He stared at me and the room became silent, quickly reaching the point at which one hears the beating of one's blood. "Yes," he said finally. "And it seems we are going to take you on."

"Now wait just a minute," I said. "Who's going to take me on?"

"New England Sensory Testing, Engineering, and Research is prepared to make you an attractive offer to function as an experimental psychologist. You will be paid handsomely and you start — immediately."

"That's wonderful," I whispered.

"We think so. NESTER — "

"NESTER?"

"Yes, New England Sensory — "

"Oh, yes . . ."

"NESTER chooses its members carefully. And once we decide, we are never wrong. You are perfect for us."

"I am?"

"Absolutely."

I gestured about the room. I touched my bruised head. "Why all of the secrecy? It's so strange."

"Oh, it's not really all that peculiar. We are an unusual operation and we must take precautions. You will understand. Later."

"I will?"

"I would hope so." He laughed. I joined him in his laughter. My heart was skipping and my head was light.

"Well," I said, "I suppose you want to know more about me." I then proceeded to describe my academic and scientific career. I explained the nature and quality of my experiments and made reference to some articles I'd published. He took all of this in with a look of utter boredom. In fact, he stared at his fingernails as I spoke.

"Yes, that's all quite fine," he said finally. "We are aware of this. But there are more important considerations. Personal considerations. We are a highly controversial organization. We require more than talent. We are interested in people with a special attitude as well. Let me ask you: Why did you answer our advertisement?"

I hemmed and hawed and tried to eke out an answer. I told him about the book clubs, about the defecating rats, about the numbing sense of insignificance I suffered from, about my desire to do something unusual and vast. There was something about his impassive eyes — they were gray and perfectly round — that goaded me.

17

I wanted him to react to what I was saying. I told him I suffered from a thwarted sense of destiny. I said things I'd never said before. Perhaps I sounded like a maniac. I told him I wanted to shape the world. I told him I was intoxicated by the thought of being part of something current. I wanted, someday, to have my name in *Newsweek*. Not on the cover. "Newsmakers" or "Transition" would be just fine. Or in *Vogue*'s "People Are Talking About." "I have the feeling," I said, "that I'll be receiving my divorce papers in the mail any day now. It would be a lot less depressing if it were newsworthy." I gave an exceedingly small laugh. "I would like to have enemies in high places," I continued. "As well as friends, of course. I would like for women who did not love me to sleep with me, if you know what I mean. Do you know what I mean?" I laughed again, more boldly this time. "I wouldn't mind being decadent," I said. "I would like for once to be in a position to renounce it all."

Robinson raised one slender finger. "Yes, yes, of course. But what is the *one* reason you wrote to us? Be singular, please."

I thought for an instant. "Power," I blurted. "I would like a little more power."

"And money?"

"Sure. Fine."

"And danger?" He leaned toward me, his eyes opening wider.

I paused. I hadn't considered it. Then it struck me that my life since I'd written to NESTER had been riddled with danger. "Why yes," I said. "Danger. Why not? Yes, that too."

18

"Good. And fame?"

"Yes, but only within a small circle. Not the matinee idol sort, nothing that would ever be put up in lights. An obscure kind of fame. Understanding my importance would be a mark of distinction."

"Naturally. Now another question — your answers are superb — what would you be willing to relinquish for all of this?"

"Relinquish?"

"Yes, of course. Do you think these things come cheaply?"

"No. Probably not. Relinquish. I don't know. I honestly can't say. I've never relinquished anything in all my life. I've lost things, things have been taken away from me. But I've never done any relinquishing . . ."

"Yes, of course. But the question, please, answer the question."

"Well, I suppose there would be very little I wouldn't give up if only a few of my dreams came true."

"Let me give you an example. If you could have these things, would you agree to never vote in another election?"

"Vote?" I laughed. "Of course I would." I continued to laugh.

Ira nodded slowly. "And would you be able to never see your current friends? To be totally cut off from them?"

"Definitely," I said, sitting up a little straighter.

"How old are you?" he asked.

"Thirty-four."

"Odd. I seem to remember in the letter you sent to us that you put your age at thirty-one."

19

"I wish that were my age."

"Your ambitions are modest, after all."

"It is one of my ambitions to have less modest ambitions."

"Yes."

"To be greater."

"Of course."

"To have more power."

"All right. Fine. And you say you are in the process of being divorced? Is that right?"

"Oh, yes."

"Any complications?"

"The usual."

"Of course. Children?"

"One. A boy. Andrew. He's eight. An adopted child."

"Admirable. You realize you may not be able to see him quite as often as you'd like to."

"It doesn't matter."

"Really. And your former wife? That doesn't matter either?"

"No, not really."

"You don't like them?"

"It's not that. It's just that we're not connected anymore. None of us really feel comfortable with each other. It becomes embarrassing."

"And your students? You won't miss them?"

"No, it's the same thing. We are too quick to sense each other's boredom. It's not real anymore."

He was lighting one cigarette with another, throwing the butts onto the floor and squashing them into the carpet with his tiny black shoes. He looked at a freshly lit

20

cigarette, put it in his mouth, sucked in deeply, and smiled at me. Then he leaned over and offered me a smoke. I accepted the cigarette. A rare gesture on my part. And felt like a blind man signing a contract. Not an unpleasant sensation.

◆ ◆ ◆

We left for the NESTER compound the next day. Ira Robinson, Factor, and Pernod had done me the favor of packing a few things from my house and there was no need to return. Everything, Ira assured me, was to be taken care of. The school administration was to be informed of my resignation. I asked Ira if the police and hospital authorities were alarmed over my disappearance, but he pretended not to hear my question. It is something I still wonder about . . .

Ira and I drove several hours in his navy blue Fiat before arriving at NESTER. He drove his little car at top speed over the frosty highway and the energetic heater steamed the windows so, I was kept busy all the time wiping them. Ira took off his handsome herringbone-tweed jacket about a hundred miles into our journey and asked me to keep it on my lap so it wouldn't wrinkle. My legs became stiff and overly warm. I tried repeatedly to engage him in conversation. I wanted to hedge my bet a little. When the idea of working for the mysterious, secret organization was first put to me I had leaped at it, but now that I had perfunctorily canceled out most of my past life I wanted to make it clear that I was merely going to check the place out, to go there on a trial basis. But Ira seemed engrossed in the radio, which he kept up at an earsplitting volume. It was rather amusing to see how familiar with popular music Ira was. Often he sang along.

Finally, we arrived. Even now, it is difficult to comprehend the nondescriptiveness of NESTER, let alone evoke it. Off the highway by only two hundred yards, the NESTER compound consists of four cream white parallelograms, each five stories high, arranged in a diamond shape. The place could have been anything: a water purification plant, the billing offices for Master Charge, an insane asylum. I wondered (and wonder still) what passing motorists must think when going by.

We entered one of the buildings through a lime green door. The interior was eerily ordinary. It looked like a fairly new high school in a lower-middle-class suburb: long, green corridors, smooth expressionless walls, an occasional porcelain drinking fountain, fire extinguishers. I stared momentarily at the rows of doors, each with a frosted glass window, each alike, each closed. Two middle-aged men, wearing lime green smocks, suddenly appeared and turned a corner. They talked to each other in low, resonant tones and then broke into gasps of repressed laughter, spluttering and choking and clapping their hands over their mouths.

I'd rather expected that Ira, or an aide, would give me a little tour of the place. You know, show me the mail room, the toilets, the cafeteria, the boss's office. But Ira, still uncommunicative, took me immediately to my office — the first hint that this was to be no cushy job. It was only a short walk to my office from the outside door, which had been triple-bolted behind us by a huge, vaguely

Oriental man. I turned with a start (my first of many) when I heard the doors being locked, and the hard, yellow man smiled unpleasantly at me.

As Ira escorted me to my office, he gave me a bit of good news. "Perhaps you are feeling that you are an ordinary employee here. I am anxious for you to know that that is untrue. There are no ordinary employees here. And you are luckier than most. We have recruits who work and live in the same room. Our quarters need expansion. You, however, will be one of the more fortunate ones. This is your office. You will work here during normal working hours. You will also be given living quarters, which I am certain you will find comfortable." He made a wave around the small, ordinary office. My eyes passed over the kidney-shaped desk, the black leather (I hoped it was leather) swivel chair, the blue two-seater couch, the goose-necked lamp, the small rectangular window with the see-through green curtains and the Venetian blinds, the beige linoleum on the floor.

Abruptly Ira left and I was alone. My life had become uncharacteristically streamlined. It seemed that just a heartbeat ago I was berating a classful of chowderheads and now I was sitting on a curious blue couch in a strange building. I tried to piece together what had passed so quickly.

Not much had happened, actually. Ira had told me very little about what I would be doing — this is not mentioned by me in defense but is simply fact and something you should know — and he had said almost nothing at all about what kind of organization NESTER was. My salary was discussed and it was to be handsome. Yes, a handsome salary. My scientific freedom was discussed and it was to be considerable. And it was made clear to me that, rather than with rats and frogs and pussy cats, I was to be experimenting with human beings.

I had fallen into a kind of reverie, trying to remember every small thing that had passed between Ira Robinson and me, and my head jerked up painfully when I heard what I thought was sobbing. A man's sobbing. I stood up and tried to discern where it was coming from. Above me? Below me? To the right? To the left? After fifteen seconds or so it stopped and there was complete and utter silence. Then I heard footsteps, hurried footsteps go past my office. And then I heard something metal drop to a floor, somewhere. And the last sound I heard before attempting to leave my office was what seemed to be a huge Chinese gong that sent reverberating bronze shivers through my body.

I wondered what was going on, even wondered, vaguely, where I was. All these sounds made me impatient with being left alone in my office and I opened the door (for a second I was afraid it would be locked) with the thought that I would take a walk, have a look around. As soon as I opened the door, however, I was met by Julius Arnold, a frog of a man, short, squat, and wearing a green blazer that fit him as tightly as a diving suit. Julius, as he was quick to tell me, was in the public relations department. He spoke quickly, jiggling his left leg as he spoke, his dark eyes almost popping out of his head. He only had a minute, he said, perhaps as reassurance, but he wanted to welcome me to NESTER. Then he gave me some pamphlets that told about the history of the organization, its aims, its achievements, and told me that there was a NESTER-wide meeting in the assembly hall in an hour. It was the first one in over six months. I must be sure to attend.

While Julius Arnold was a far from attractive figure, his brief visit made me feel much better and I spent the next hour studying the literature he left with me. I assumed my position behind my desk, which at that time did not wobble, and read the pamphlets with great care, underlining sentences of particular interest. (I am always like that in new situations, meticulous, optimistic, enthusiastic. For instance, when I was in school, the highlight of the semester would always be the buying of new texts and new loose-leaf notebooks. I would pat them, sign them, put them in perfect order, ready for the months ahead. After that it was all downhill.) The pamphlets were vague but well done. NESTER, I noted, was born in 1904 (the same year, I remembered, that Pavlov received the Nobel Prize). It had been a small organization, cloistered and secret. The literature was so vague that I only got glimmerings of facts that flashed like little golden fish in murky waters. NESTER, it said, had always been a secret organization. That much I knew before. It was one of the main attractions. It was secret, slightly subterranean, but authoritative, well financed. I loved that. The real meat of the literature was an explanation of why they couldn't say anything substantive in the pamphlets. They could, they said, show pictures of the numerous recreational facilities, the sophisticated scientific technology, the living quarters, the officers . . . but it would be an unnecessary risk of the security and tranquillity of the NESTER compound, the NESTER quest.

I leaned back in my swivel chair — glad to see that it did not tip and lurch as my chair at the university had — and took quiet pleasure in my new job. I was certain of having made a brilliant choice. I thought of NESTER being secret — how nice that was. Secret. Shhh, don't tell anyone but I'm revolutionizing the world. Oh, that was pleasing.

Soon there was a knock at the door and old Julius Arnold, accompanied by the man I was later to know as Tom Simon, was there to take me to the auditorium.

During the short walk we, or rather they, talked excitedly about a new kind of exercise belt that was supposed to take an inch a day off one's waistline. They had heard of and tried many such belts but this particular one was supposed to be the finest, it was actually supposed to work.

The auditorium was huge, with a domed green ceiling. Instinctively, I put my hand to my throat as I entered. The air was cold, very cold. There were hundreds of souls there, coming from all walks of life. Some looked like finicky, asthmatic geniuses, others had the bearings of plumbers or trapeze artists. All, I assumed, were necessary and, in their own way, deserved to be there.

The seats were made of stone. Long white stone benches that had been carved in rows accommodated thirty people with proper indentations where one actually sat. I was charmed at the sight of them but, as I mentioned, it was very chilly in that huge domed room and sitting on stone tended to make matters worse.

The auditorium was filled nearly to capacity, so Julius, Tom, and myself had to sit separately. I found a single space near the front. To my left was a huge, red-haired, very mild looking man wearing a green jumpsuit with NESTER embroidered over his breast pocket. On my right was a rather beautiful young woman wearing outrageous quantities of make-up and a pigeon-foot-pink mini skirt from which her ample legs rushed in all their fuzzy splendor. It was amusing to survey the room and see who my fellow NESTER-ites were. I decided to turn around and take a good look at whoever it was that sat behind me — I had picked up some of his conversation and he seemed to be talking about DNA, my old specialty. But as I turned, the lights went out suddenly and I, along with everyone else, was cast into darkness.

We all stayed like that, cast into darkness, for a good minute and a half. Then thick green curtains parted at the front of the auditorium, revealing a supernaturally white movie screen. Music filled the hall, a joyful crescendo of trumpets and violins. What followed was a fairly routine, almost tedious film that extolled the wonders of NESTER. There were charts whose thrusting upward lines clearly described the remarkable financial progress of the organization. There were brief statements made by two members of the previous Presidential cabinet in which they commended NESTER's work and looked forward to the day when such an organization could exist openly in our great nation. (This wafted an audible *oooooh* through the enthralled hundreds.) What else? There were pictures of the location where the NESTER compound now sat, pictures taken before the buildings had been erected. A field of grass, the crumbling remains of an ancient well, a skinny red dog that nosed around worrisomely. "And out of this . . ." the narrator extolled, and next we were presented with a picture of the cream white compound that we now lived in, as if it had been inexplicably beckoned by the moon.

Soon, if not soon enough, the movie ended and the lights in the auditorium were restored. Over the speakers that had carried the music and the soundtrack of the film, a voice announced: "Ladies and gentlemen, Mr. Ira Robinson." There was a very warm burst of applause.

"Well," began Ira with a folksiness that rather surprised me, "I see a lot of familiar faces here. I'm always glad for these get-togethers. It's good to have a chance, once in a while, for us to see who we are." (I straightened up in my seat and pushed my chin forward. I hoped, for some reason, that Ira would look at me as he spoke. I felt a little isolated.) "Now the dynamics of our organization here doesn't allow us to really get to know each other and, in the course of your hardworking and demanding days, some of you may lose sight of the fact that this is a large group of people working together toward a goal. So I thought we would all just sound off and introduce ourselves. Let's just start from the front here: stand up, tell us your name and where you work. I guess it'll be a little hard to keep track since there's so many of us, but I think it'll help." He pointed to an elderly, very fat man in a white suit. "Bill, why don't you start off?"

For the next forty-five minutes, two hundred of the chosen stood up and screamed out their names.

♦　♦　♦

That was a long time ago and I wish to repent. I am a brain thief and I am no kid. My heart is heavy, my step slow; I am no kid. I am ahead of my time and request, sir, permission to sit down while the rest of the world catches up. I am the evil genius. I am the Enigma of the Airport. I am Sea to Shining Sea Man. Come here my lovelies and look. I am the rain beating on the roof.

2

SOON, SOON ENOUGH I will leak my secrets. It is about ten in the evening now, as I sit writing furtively, fearsomely into this thick notebook with thin lined paper. On the outskirts of the city . . . The city? I've neglected to mention where I'm living now — these security precautions I promised to observe when I first began this confession interest me less and less. NESTER and I are located several miles outside Boston, Massachusetts. Perhaps you've guessed. Or perhaps these memoirs are already common knowledge as you read them. Or perhaps I've been found face down and bloated, floating in the filthy Charles River, an unknown man. Or perhaps I've had a burst of drunken courage and sold this searing exposé to the Public Broadcasting Corporation and have been a key witness in some spectacular Senate investigation. (Though I think this unlikely. Who in the Senate would dare expose my superiors? Even if I would.) What I really plan to do is smuggle this confession into, say,

30

northern Europe, contact some courageous publisher, and have it printed under an assumed name. Then . . . then I will be hidden in the Danish woods, hosted gloriously by a beautiful blond ex-socialist, to whom I shall teach English. But there will only be momentary repose and for years, forever, my life will be a series of disappearances and reappearances along a vast network of underground railways, always in the loving, carnal care of people who admire my selfless sacrifice of personal safety. ("Personal safety," I will say, and make an ambiguous gesture.)

Now, so I will deserve the hoopla I like to think awaits me, I will tell you a little about how NESTER works. It's really quite extraordinary in some aspects. In others it's as banal as the Gestapo. We employ phone taps, we intercept mail, we spy with high-powered telescopes, we employ an unscrupulous dentist who puts radio transmitters in certain patients' fillings. We wear tan trench coats and follow people down crowded boulevards, we rub up against them in rush hour subways, we panhandle them, we falsely represent charitable organizations and solicit people right in their own living rooms. We pose as insurance and reference book salesmen, we dress up as scout masters and try to sell raffle-tickets, we pose in official uniforms of all sorts — anything to get to people and do our nasties. We even have brief, unbelievably intense affairs with them, if necessary.

Less banal than this, we have our crews of reality synthesizers: the camera and sound crew, those celluloid ghosts, those human shadows. Our understanding of a subject is based largely on the raw material presented us by the film crew. It is quite interesting and very valuable

31

for us to see how the subject walks, gestures, sits, smiles, sleeps, defecates, makes love, jumps back in total terror. We become used to him. He becomes part of our world, our mythic present. In some cases, in the peculiar glow of our offices, he becomes our best friend, the object of our most baroque passions.

The third point in NESTER's six-prong fork is the surgical team. NESTER surgery is done in some undesignated place — but sometimes a low moan, a squeal, or even a deafening antiseptic hush makes me believe the operations are taking place right here, beneath me, or above me, or is it there, behind some hidden panel, some sliding door. The surgeons are the most hideous and necessary part of the NESTER approach to information seeking, for without their insertion of the microelectrode, without their utterly scientific snooping and snipping, without their stereotaxic wizardry, we would be without the necessary neuronal data. We would be, in short, out of business.

The surgeons would have no one to operate on (think of it!) were it not for our fourth division, the Force Recruiters. This collection of paroled criminals, ex-prize fighters, wildly aggressive immigrants, and ex-servicemen is trained by our Violence Coordinator, NESTER's laconic label for perky Miss Mitchell whom, as you know, I would like to lay. The Force Recruiters, or, as the cafeteria comedians sometimes call them, the Heavies, capture our chosen subjects and bring them to us for the simple, very simple, quick, very quick, painless, entirely painless insertion. They bring them to us. For the insertion. They hit them on the top (or, perhaps, the side) of the head and stuff the limp, soon to be violated body into a long

32

black car, which in some cases is dark maroon. The Heavies, while unquestionably loyal to NESTER, exhibit unconcealed contempt for everyone else in the organization, except the men at the very top, whoever they may be.

After the microelectrode is placed in the subject's brain, he is hypnotized and all memory traces of the brief trauma are erased. The hypnotists act as a liaison between the surgeons, Heavies, and my slice of the NESTER pie, the psychologists. (The hypnotists, or the Trauma Erasers, do an impeccable job of concealing from the conscious mind what has befallen the brain; but good hypnotists are few and in most cases we are left with no other recourse but to blot out the incident by giving the subject a rather pungent dose of electroconvulsive shock.)

While my specialty is experimental psychology, the scientific portion of NESTER cannot be contained by any one discipline. We have some of the most prominent behaviorists in the world, more than one Zen psychiatrist, an old student of Jung, dozens of psychoanalysts of Freudian or Adlerian persuasions, neurochemists, and a French pharmacologist who was hired especially to deal with euphoric drugs with which we can introduce microelectrodes into the brains of younger subjects, thus saving us the expense of surgery. It is our collective function to give meaning to the vast bulk of data coming from our subject's brain. In some cases we may be analyzing changing resting axon potentials, or we may be doing a quick run-down of the somatic sensory system, or comparisons of photo pigments — or we may deal with less technical information like conversations, photographs,

33

slips of the tongue. While we can tell whether a particular dream our subject is having is pleasant or not, we cannot, with any great confidence, ascertain the exact content of the dream. Dream language is too idiosyncratic, too personal. However, when the subject becomes familiar enough to us, certain educated guesses can be made. So to my way of thinking, we are the most important part of the outfit, the most diversified. (Even in the midst of my revulsion I cannot contain my insane pride.)

The sixth prong is the computer boys, who, like the rest of us, consider themselves the most important part of NESTER. I see the computer as a bank that saves what the rest of us earn, and it is only a certain Calvinist craziness that leads some to believe that the saving of a thing is more important than the thing itself. But I can't blame those nice crew cuts for feeling the way they do about their giant machine, for it is conceivably the finest ever built. It extrapolates and reclassifies as fast as a rabbit's heartbeat and is wired with more interconnections than the human brain — which is saying quite a bit, since there are about twelve billion nerve cells in a man's brain and the possible interconnections between them are greater than all of the atomic particles in the universe.

Actually, there is a seventh division in the organization, NESTER's "apostrophes," as it were. These are the miscellaneous employees, who are, in fact, the largest single group. They are technicians and assistants. The disgruntled housewife who now reads an oscilloscope, the Hungarian handwriting expert who used to work in nightclubs, several feisty old Irishmen who work as guards. We have a middle-aged woman who, I'm told, is a disciple of

B. F. Skinner and who runs experiments on specially bred rodents to see if the data we've robbed from our human subjects can be used to predict animal behavior. Someone, somewhere, has designs on everything that breathes. Aside from these people, the "apostrophes" consists of field representatives, who recruit new talent into the fold and sell NESTER's services to dignitaries of all kinds — congressmen, chairmen of the board, manufacturers, foreigners, anyone who'll pay. Also in this category are the administrators, the supervisors, the cafeteria help, the scrubwomen, paymaster, secretaries — all carefully chosen, all security-checked, all with life-time contracts. Whether they know it or not.

So that's how it works. It may not mean too much to you now. A little abstract, but you get the drift. Sleuths, camera and sound crews, surgeons, Force Recruiters, scientists, computer programmers and operators, and the possessives. As you have already discovered, the purpose of NESTER is to get inside — deep inside — the human brain. Oh, poor delicate little beast! We pierce the pons, maul the medulla, heist the hypothalamus. Object: control. Object: manipuation. Object: power. They are brain thieves and I wish to repent.

♦ ♦ ♦

For my first two months here I was a Missing Person, but now I am dead. As soon as NESTER was certain my talents were valuable they killed me. I have been buried, lightly eulogized, briefly mourned, and virtually forgotten. This little prank is played on most of us here. I was aware of this possibility about a week after moving in, but

I figured my life on the outside had been so uncompli-
cated, so barren, that it wouldn't be necessary in my case.

Apparently, it was necessary. It was nothing they discussed with me, nothing we planned together. One day,
over coffee in a Styrofoam cup, I was reading the Boston
Globe and I noticed my name on page 11.

UNIVERSITY PROF DEAD
IN STORROW CRASH

A man identified as Paul Galambos, a professor of
psychology at ⸺ University in ⸺, was
found early this morning near the Mystic Bridge.
He was alone in a car that apparently had gone out
of control. Although the body was badly burned,
positive identification was made through Mr. Galambos' documents which escaped the flames that
engulfed him and his late model car. Mr. Galambos
had been reported missing from the ⸺ Hospital, where he disappeared more than two months
ago. He was in the hospital being treated for inju-
ries sustained during a fall.

I was furious. I went straight to Mr. Worthington, who
turned out not to be so inaccessible after all, and, waving
the newspaper in his face, I demanded to know why I was
dead, why I had not been consulted, why why why.

"It is common procedure," he said, with an elegant
wave. "And your wife had hired a private detective to
look for you."

"She had?" I found that hard to believe.

"That also is common procedure." He smiled.

"I don't believe Lydia would spend a dime looking
for me," I blurted, resting my hand on his gleaming desk.

36

"That is a conundrum you are free to pursue on your own time," he answered coldly. He glanced at my hand as if it were something he planned to wipe off his desk. Then he looked at me. "Oh, but look how unhappy you are," he crooned. He rose from his deep chair and walked over to me. He clapped his hand on my shoulder and then sat on the edge of his desk. He crossed his legs — a slash of white appeared between his pants cuff and the tops of his black socks. "Look at the positive side," he suggested. "You are now more firmly than ever a member of our team. We have already raised your pay scale. You can double-check this with accounts, but I believe something on the order of three hundred and fifty more dollars a month are being put into your account. And there'll be another salary review in three months. Three months! Not a year, not six months. Not bad, hmmm?" He slid off the desk and walked around his office, shaking his narrow shoulders within his plush blue jacket. "We don't ask you to join us in discovering a new world so we can make your life unpleasant. Your life is, I trust, quite pleasant. And as you become more used to it and become richer and better at your work, your life will increase in its pleasantness. You are already what is known as a well-to-do man. You are paid handsomely and your expenses are virtually nonexistent. Someday you will be rich. Perhaps you will take your money one day and live in a foreign country — I often think of it for myself — at which time you will be uncommonly rich. But that isn't all, is it? You are gaining knowledge. You are on board a ship of destiny. A marvelous and unheard-of adventure. We are making everything obsolete. We are discovering America."

He stood now in front of me and rested his pale spotted hand on my shoulder. "That's what we're doing. Discovering America, brain by brain."

I didn't tell him that money meant increasingly less and less to me. I visited the city once a month, and then I was with three or four other colleagues; we had to stick together and it was rare indeed that I had a chance to spend my money. No, I did not tell him that. I stopped waving the newspaper. I asked if my mother had been informed. Mr. Worthington nodded, yes. I asked after a few more people. Then I asked if I might attend my funeral.

He laughed softly. "So many ask that," he said in a dreamy voice. Then, switching to a far more specific tone: "We've traced it to a childhood dream common in many of — us. To attend one's own funeral. To share in the mourning. To ascertain the loyalty of various friends. To hear what is said."

"Well, may I?" I asked, feeling like that childish dreamer.

"Negative on that one, Paul. Far too risky. If you were spotted — I mean, after all, what would people think?"

"If I gave a good goddamn about what people thought," said I, "then I most likely wouldn't be here in the first place. Right?"

"You're learning," said Mr. W. with a fond smile. "You're getting there, just catching on, you are."

"Learning what?" I asked, feeling suddenly puzzled and out of my depth.

"Why," he answered with a rare reverberation of nerves beneath his voice, "learning. Learning, that's all. Learn-

38

ing who you are, what you can and cannot do, learning why you're here."

"I'm here to do experiments," I said, still tense with desire to attend my funeral. "I'm here because I answered your advertisement."

"Yes. Well, whatever you say." He stood up, obviously preparing to dismiss me. He looked at me with concern and deep impersonality, as if the latest stock market quotations were at that moment being flashed across my forehead.

"Why are you looking at me?" I said, feeling snappish beyond words.

"Quite simply, because I like you."

"You do?" I said in an attempt to prolong our conference.

"Yes, quite a bit. You are a deeply bitter man, filled with . . ." His voice trailed off. He turned away and his eyes caught a bit of artificial light that made them look like stones.

"Filled with what?" I asked, uncomfortable with the sound of my voice.

"Passion," he said, turning toward me. His eyes fixed upon mine and he folded his hands.

"It's true," I said, turning quickly away.

"That makes you unusual here, then. Most of our people are men and women who have had passion and sorrow bred out of them at a surprisingly early age. I mean, let's face it, our business here is not altogether a kind one. No matter what we think the final goals may be, what we are doing now on a day-to-day basis leaves, morally speaking, something to be desired. Hmmm?"

39

"I don't know. It's not something which I find useful or productive to think about. I leave speculations about morality to the specialists," I said with a hollow laugh.

Mr. Worthington moved close to me and put his hand on my shoulder. "I am something of a specialist in these matters," he said. "And I will be paying particular attention to you, just from precisely that perspective."

I didn't know what the hell he was talking about and, frankly, it would have been difficult for me to care less. "Why can't I go to my funeral?" I said. "I'll be quite careful. I'll wear a disguise. I'll stay as far away as possible. There's really no risk."

"Then why wouldn't I just let you go? Do you think I like to argue with you?"

"No, I don't. But it's just that — "

"Well, all right," he interrupted, "then go. Just be careful. I'll make arrangements."

"Really?"

"I like to change my mind," he said.

Indeed he does. The promise to let me attend my funeral was broken. When I think of how happy I was as he showed me out, how I smiled with canine gratitude as he handed me a mint and patted my shoulder, I want to scream. For on the day I was to be buried, three of my subjects reportedly began to exhibit irrational eating behavior — one of them gaining eight pounds in thirty-six hours — and I was told by Tom Simon, a middle-management moron if one ever breathed, that my services would be required all day Sunday. Brains, he said, don't take holidays and neither do their watchers. I protested. I protested greatly. I said it was unfair. Said I'd been promised. Called him a cheat. The works. No avail. And so, as I was being lowered into the cold cold ground — they'd taken "my remains" back to Pennsylvania, to my hometown choking darkly in the plundered hills — I was engrossed in the ventromedial nucleus of a dude ranch owner living on the outskirts of Albuquerque, New Mexico, and I felt a sorrow as long and as lonely as Route 66.

♦ ♦ ♦

Now this compound of cream white buildings encompasses my entire life. I have been removed from the human alphabet. No friends, no neighbors, I am isolated in the extreme, an unwilling hermit, a martyr without faith. After a full day in my office juggling data, comparing tests, writing reports, and reading other people's mail, I have dinner with three fellow NESTER-oids in the dining room (in the afternoon we call it the cafeteria) and then come here to my living quarters. My quarters are small but not cramped. I have a window that looks out onto the concrete courtyard. No, there are no machine gunners, no goose-stepping guards, no barbed wire, no inquisitive finger of light leafing through the darkness every thirty seconds. There is, instead, nothing. Nothing, simply nothing. There is a profusion of concrete, but that is of course nothing. There are, to the extreme left, several dozen parked cars, but they are also nothing. Over there to the right is a huge electrical generator, painted orange, which because of its color may be something, but when it is dark, as it is now, it is for all practical purposes nothing. Across the courtyard are a dozen or so separate

41

squares of light, the windows of other NESTER employees not yet asleep, but since I don't know who they are they are also nothing, nothing, zero.

I pace my room, switching on and off the electrical gadgets that have been granted me. The television, the radio, the stereo set, toaster, blender, coffee maker, and another toaster that doesn't work. My room is pleasant and normal in the extreme. No clashing colors, no harsh angles, a more than full liquor cabinet, a brilliant mirror attached to the inside of the closet door.

But despite the fringe benefits involved in being a brain thief, I have become, in the past couple of months, more and more unhappy here, more and more determined to leave. My feelings of claustrophobia — difficult to handle even in my previous life — have mounted uncontrollably here and together with the fact that I can never go out act as a constant irritant on my nervous system. I am now earning a fabulous salary, none of which I ever see. The only time I ever actually touch money is on the infrequent days I am taken to Boston on a group excursion, and then it is a very small amount. But I wouldn't mind *that* so much if it weren't for the insecurity. It's really impossible for me to speak to anyone here. During my *very infrequent* meetings with certain fellow employees who have been assigned to me as social partners, I feel that my every joke is being scrutinized for treasonous nuances. The fact is that it would be pathetically easy for the Boys Upstairs to have my life completely monitored — after all, it is their stock and trade.

There are benefits, however. As I sit here in my room, watching the nonexistent windows across the courtyard blacken one by one by three by four by two, until only I and one other tortured soul remain awake, I ask myself if I am still haunted by the heartbreaking sense of obscurity that prompted me to seek out NESTER in the first place and the answer is no. Even though *Newsweek* has yet to mention (or even hint at) my name and *Vogue* has neither complimented nor ridiculed my sense of style, I no longer carry with me that dreadful sense of unimportance. There are no more pimply girl cashiers in poorly stocked bookstores to treat me like everyone else, no gas station attendants whose gaze drifts uncaringly past me as they hastily wipe my windshield, no gummy waitresses to take my order as if it couldn't matter less. My life no longer has that dissipated, arbitrary, thin feeling. My days are dense, my work important. And though we here at NESTER treat each other with an enforced air of impersonality, there lingers even in the anonymity a sultry significance.

◆ ◆ ◆

I am playing with fire. Since beginning this notebook I have been feeling the walls moving in. For months my loathing of this place has swum along the bottom of my heart like one of those blind scavenger fish that patrols the floor of the ocean at its deepest points. But now that I am beginning to articulate my mangled feelings about this, the grossest error of my faltering life, my ill will toward NESTER and practically everything about it has grown astronomically.

But at the same time — and this is strange to me — my position here becomes more and more respected. You see, I am good at my work, very good. Promotions loom on the near horizon. Who am I to complain? I'll take everything they care to give. I'll learn all I can. But in my case it will be different. Every other boob here plans to remain locked behind these doors for the rest of his life. As for me, I will own up to my mistakes. I will take my leave in the dead of night. And repent. I'll take my chances. It will be a renunciation of Biblical proportions. I'll blow this joint sky-high. Perhaps it will be necessary for me to spend a little time behind bars, though I doubt that. All the rest of them, however. Yes, they will be imprisoned. They will be held without bail, no visitors allowed, given speedy and secret trials, perhaps roughed up a little bit. Why not? This is surely an unforgivable claque of satans. Meanwhile I will have slipped from the tortured shores of this land, aboard a blinding white steamer due in Copenhagen in eight or nine days, depending on the weather.

◆ ◆ ◆

My experiments with eating behavior seem to be coming toward some fruitful conclusion. As you may or may not know, things like the stomach or the taste buds have little to do with how much or when we eat — in fact we can remove them and eating behavior remains constant. Like everything else, eating or not eating is controlled by the brain. The part that interests us most here is the area around the lateral hypothalamus. Take a rat or a Russian, a tap dancer, a turkey, it doesn't matter, almost any living thing, and stimulate the lateral hypothalamus and you will get — presto! — eating be-

44

havior. The system that causes us to eat is always on. It's a freewheeling center that needs no encouragement. The only reason we don't occupy every waking movement with eating is that when we have had enough, which is to say when our jaws are sufficiently exercised, our gut filled, and our blood-sugar level up to an acceptable count, another system switches on which inhibits the "feed me feed me" beeps of the lateral hypothalamus. This satiety center is the ventromedial nucleus.

Anything that is done in nature can be done experimentally. Weeks ago I postulated a certain chemical additive that could be introduced tastelessly into food and would systematically inhibit the firing of the ventromedial nucleus. Eating a food so treated would actually make you hungrier than when you started. Eat a pound and you'd be famished. If you didn't wise up and switch to some other snack you could conceivably pass out in an oversatiated stupor. You can easily imagine what the commercial possibilities are.

Unfortunately, our subjects were gaining enormous amounts of weight — four pounds a day wasn't unusual — and the ethical/practical problems of heart attacks and insanity presented themselves. Then I had the perfectly obvious idea of putting the ventromedial nucleus inhibitor in a very low calorie food. Admittedly, we are a little worried about the effects of this — in a meeting yesterday morning, attended by only a select few, Mr. Worthington himself said we were worried — but a major food product company has just bought the formula and intermediate data from us for millions.

"But why stop at commerce?" I asked. Mr. Worthington

stood on the slightly raised stage, charts and graphs hanging behind him, his spotted white hands oddly striped by the podium's small lamp. The light in the small conference room was dim and I couldn't read his expression. I did, however, sense the proximity of lunchtime and I sensed also the impatience of my colleagues. "Why stop at commerce?" I repeated the question and rose to my feet. "Couldn't we use our increased power over the hypothalamus as a way of solving some of the world's conflicts? Starvation, for instance. If we can turn the ventromedial nucleus off, we can turn it on, and keep whole impoverished nations in a state of satiety. No more hunger. Ever. Man's oldest dream. I realize we could have fed the world's hungry millions a long time ago with no problem, but it was believed — and rightly so — that when a subjugated people rise above the starvation level they use the increased energy in very destructive ways, such as revolution or other forms of uncontrolled violence. But with the distribution of free food that would give no real nutrition, and so no new strength, but would significantly tone down the hypothalamus' hunger signals, we could alleviate much of the grumbling discontent that so plagues many parts of the world and further insure the smooth, peaceful running of society. I think India would be interested in this, Red China, Arkansas. Really, everyone has this problem to a certain extent, except perhaps a few countries in northern Europe."

There were eleven of us at the meeting. I'd say about three felt any enthusiasm about my idea. Most everyone here is either interested in pure research or in strictly commercial ideas —concepts of long range and absolute control appeal only to a few. There were a few stray comments, an irrelevant question, and then we were dismissed. I was feeling pretty low until Mr. Worthington called out to me. I went to his side and stood there as he put twenty-five or so yellow sheets of note paper back into his pigskin briefcase. Then he looked up at me with a wink. "Brilliant," he said. "Simply brilliant. Don't let those guys bother you too much," he said, jerking his head toward the semicircle of vacated folding chairs. "They work for me."

◆ ◆ ◆

Rather than take lunch, I went to my room and changed into my sneakers, gray T-shirt, supporter, and maroon gym shorts. I packed a little shaving bag with a tube of shampoo, a bar of glycerine soap, and a can of deodorant and went to the exercise room (Fitness Chamber). Lacking the courage to face the olfactory affront of the cafeteria, whose air was rife with air-conditioning and turkey noodle casserole, I thought I might work out. There was a tension in me that asserted itself as a stiffness of muscle, a tightness of throat, a brittleness of spine, and I thought that twenty minutes of semistrenuous activity might help to relieve it.

There was something in Mr. Worthington's eyes when he said, "They work for me," that had dosed my already staggering nervous system with 30 ccs of strangeness and fear. Yes, there are times when old Mr. W. seems scarcely human to me, times when his manner is deeply, abhorrently ironic, as if he were watching me with the same mixture of amusement, eagerness, and utter objectivity

47

that yours truly has shown watching an experimental rat or, most recently, a Rotarian.

Guarding the entrance to the gymnasium was a man named Eddie Marshall, whom everyone called Cookie, or so he told me. He sat in a gray folding chair near the door, with a folding table piled with clean towels next to him and his short, chunky legs crossed. The first time I made use of the gym he did his best to entangle me in the vines and quicksand of his overheated conversation — he was less suited for a solitary life than any man I had ever met — and this time I was careful not to engage his eyes as I grabbed a rough little towel and made my way into the gym. "How long you going to be?" he asked me in his lonely, wet voice. I shrugged.

The Fitness Chamber is small. There is, above it, a nicely banked track, one tenth of a mile around. In a corner there are some rubber mats and barbells. There are a couple of sets of parallel bars — in the entire course of my life I have never so much as touched a parallel bar. There is a stationary bicycle upon which one has the option of pumping with all of one's might and going nowhere — perhaps the most arty and existential of all exercises. There is a sandbag with the features of a human drawn upon it which is sometimes punched and sometimes attacked with a long stick. There is also a half basketball court, where I chose to take my exercise. A red basketball had rolled into a corner and I shagged it — *pat pat pat* echoed my floppy sneaks across the varnished yellow floor. I dribbled the ball — it sounded like gunshots in a canyon — and moved across the court. Rising momentarily onto my toes, I tossed the ball at the

48

basket; the ball hit the metal hoop and bounced back in my direction. I ran over to catch it — *pat pat pat.* I dribbled toward the basket (*pat pat bang bang*) and tried a lay-up shot. I could already feel a pleasant trickle of sweat in the small of my back. The ball touched nothing when I tossed it up — rather surprising and faintly disheartening, since I was only three feet from the basket. It hit the floor with a sharp warlike crack and, as I raced over to catch it before it rolled away, I noticed that I was not alone.

There, in a dark blue suit, leaning against the door with his hands behind his back, was Mr. Worthington. His snowy eyebrows were highly arched, his lips pressed tightly together, as if he might be considering me for the second string of an intra-NESTER basketball squad. When he saw that I had noticed him, his aspect changed with a speed and thoroughness that was more than a little unnerving and he was smiling at me with that chilling guilelessness I had previously associated only with Eisenhower and my maternal grandfather. "What ho! Mr. Worthington," I called, sending a bounce pass his way. He caught the spinning red ball in two hands, lifted it chest high and jiggled it for a moment as if he were estimating the ball's weight. He bounced it back in my general direction — I had to lunge, in fact to prevent it skipping past me — and he walked toward me, his old spotted hands now folded monkishly in front of him.

"What ho, Paul," he said softly, molding his voice precisely to the dimensions of the room, like a cardinal murmuring vespers in a cathedral.

Unsure why he was with me, I bounced the ball back

to him. He caught it on the first hop and, in one easy motion, tossed it into the hoop, a perfect swish that scarcely disturbed the netting. The ball smacked to the floor. "What brings you?" I asked, watching the ball bounce, first energetically, then lazily, and then exhaustedly.

He answered with what seemed an obvious lie. "I often come here."

I didn't pursue it — he was certainly not dressed for the exercise room, but pointing this out would not have been wise.

"Do you come here often?" he asked, still smiling.

"This is my second time," I answered in utter frankness.

"It's important to keep in shape," said Mr. W., "and it's important to relax. The Fitness Chamber is a good place to accomplish both. Get the ball."

Expressing what glimmer of independence I felt in his presence with a quick shrug, I shagged the ball. "Let's see it," he said, clapping his hands. In my nervousness, I threw the ball past him. He shook his head and chased it down as it thundered haphazardly against the back wall. He caught the ball and slapped at it until it bounced coherently. Then, taking it in both hands, he tossed it underhand the length of the small court and it fell through the hoop. "Hey!" he called. "Not bad!"

I retrieved the ball and, not wishing to be outdone but aware that I had been, tried an impossible hook shot, lofting the ball over my left shoulder with my back to the basket — better to miss a tricky shot than to muff an easy one. The neutral red ball hit the top of the backboard with a dreadful *thwang*.

"What kind of shot is that?" asked Worthington, tracking down the ball. "Why is it that when things get difficult people want to surrender all control?"

"I'm sure I don't know," I answered.

After a moment's harshness, his features were once again benign. "Well," he said, tossing the ball in front of him and catching it between his outspread palms, "These are the kinds of questions I often ask myself." He feinted a shot at the basket and quickly passed the ball to me, bouncing it off my chest. "Sorry," he said expressionlessly, retrieving. Walking toward me, the ball tucked under his arm — straining the button on his suit nearly to the bursting point — he indicated a wooden bench near the barbells and said, "Let's sit down for a minute."

I walked a respectful and involuntary half pace behind him, wondering if the old man was going to require me to perform feats of strength with the ponderous black weights. A brief fantasy of being pinned red-faced and hysterical beneath the malice of a quarter-ton barbell and Mr. Worthington leaning forward on the bench saying, "Now lean into it, boy. Give it all you have."

"I don't believe in weightlifting," I said, as soon as we sat down.

Mr. Worthington nodded vacantly and said, "Oh."

Compulsively pressing my disadvantage, I continued in the same vein. "Weightlifting develops the muscles in unnatural and useless ways. I find bulging muscles disgusting. They restrict movement and the moment you stop working out they turn to blubber."

"Don't worry," Mr. W. said.

"What shouldn't I worry about?" I countered, ever vigilant.

"Your duties don't include the lifting of weights," he said with a knowing laugh. "In fact, I'm surprised you make use of our exercise facilities. Quite surprised."

"I used to jog."

"Did you?" he asked. He seemed as if he were truly surprised, as if I'd told him I once taught sky diving. "What else did you use to do?"

"Sit-ups, from time to time." I slapped my spongy gut.

"Did you ever read the Bible?" he asked, leaning forward and resting his chin in a spidery bridge of locked fingers.

"When I was an undergraduate I took a course in the Bible as Literature."

"Did you? Now, that's fascinating." He straightened up and leaned back. He rolled his eyes toward the ceiling and, stretching his slender legs in front of him, crossed his ankles. "Did you ever notice how different the Biblical conception of an angel is from our own?"

"I don't have much conception of angels," I said with a hint of sarcasm and languor.

"Oh, of course you do. What do you think of when you think of an angel?"

I felt the kind of fear and impatience at his questions one might feel upon being accosted by a violent stranger with a terrible stutter. "I don't know," I said. Was he trying to press my already overtaxed imagination to the limits? I wondered. "I think of . . . some drag queen with a muslin gown and a lute."

"That's the best you can do?"

I closed my eyes. "Or a beautiful, tall woman — a Dane or something — with heavy robes and a dove perched on her arm."

"And is she kind?" he asked in a tight little voice, grasping my arm.

I almost fell off the bench. "Yes, yes," I said, practically giggling with embarrassment and fear. There was no doubt in my mind that I was the fool in some elaborate trick.

"You see?" he said, clasping his hands together and smiling. "This is a wholly contemporary conception. A mixture of cartoons and greeting cards. But in olden times an angel was no soft-hearted spirit, no fairy godmother. Angels, Paul, are terrible. They are most awful things. That business about terrible swift swords is much more like it than harps and halos. Read your Bible. Or any real spiritual document. Most cases of divine intervention have been anything but comfortable for the humans who have been involved. Angels are usually illogical and harsh." He fell suddenly silent.

"I didn't know you were a student of religion," I said after some time had passed.

Mr. Worthington looked quickly at me, as if I had disturbed a reverie. "Hmmm?"

"I didn't know you were a student of religion," I said, having no choice but to repeat what I wished I hadn't said in the first place.

He shrugged. "Well, I should think you know very little about me, Paul," he said. He slapped his knees and stood up. He glanced at the sloping track above us and ran his tongue over his back teeth. And for one ice-cold, numinous moment I expected him to spread his old arms and, with a toss of his head and a flutter of feet, rise to the rubber runway like a long gray balloon. My hands clenched the edge of the bench. I felt way out of my depth, like a man in a rented rowboat in the middle of the ocean. I wished I were alone. I felt awkward and thick and ungainly.

He turned slowly toward me and said, "Well, I've got to toddle along now."

3

I WANT EVERYTHING on my own terms. As a child in
Pennsylvania I would stare hatefully at my teachers,
longing for the day when I could sit behind one of those
big blond desks and make a new generation of students
as miserable as I was being made. Years later, I was
teaching psychology in a very expensive center of higher
learning and feeling that my goals had been puny and
undistinguished. It was then that my mind began to drift
toward the grandiose. I considered spying, advertising,
show business, remarriage to an exotic woman, really anything that might make my life more distinctive, unique.
Then, of course, along came NESTER and I opted for
that . . .

Anyhow, the conquest of space has left mankind in a
particularly demoralized state of mind. An interesting
phrase: state of mind. As if consciousness were a government, sending out edicts to the subservient senses. It is,
as a matter of fact, as difficult to alter consciousness as

it is to upset a political or social order, and the aftermath is equally authoritarian. And the labor pains as mankind ambles toward extinction . . . you must, please, forgive this babbling but, and here I must write with my pen just barely touching the paper, there is someone outside my door. I'm sure of it. A foot scrapes. Heavy breathing. As I was saying, nostalgia is a sexual problem. Time, of course, is a sea serpent swallowing itself. Remember? Don't you recall? These are things about which we both agree. You and I, Contessa. We have spent a lovely amber afternoon discussing these matters . . .

They've left. My heart leaps and beats like an untamed beast in a prison of bone. I am being spied upon. Some supersonic sleuth is detecting my pen's scratching across these pages and he is attempting to decipher the treasonous content of my words. Excuse me for a moment while I collect myself, have a drink, take off my maroon silk robe which hangs so limply over my body, in mourning for its lost belt. Quite a nice robe, really. These mail-order houses aren't half-bad.

I'm back. I've been away longer than the proximity of these paragraphs suggests. Had that drink and another. Sat on the edge of my bed. Rocking. My head in my hands. Knowing that somewhere in the awfulness of this compound I was being tapped, taped, and tabulated. Oh, the old Triple T! I ransacked my room, looking for, perhaps, a hidden microphone. A tiny, tucked-away tape recorder. A concealed camera. Any evidence that I was being spied upon. I tore off my bedspread, emptied my dresser drawers, shook out an entire tin of talcum powder . . .

Now it's late, very late. I must be at work in five hours. I am pulling at my hair. There must be something I can do. Perhaps the gymnasium is still open and I can take a sauna bath or swim some laps in the bluest pool I have ever seen. Or perhaps I'll check into the infirmary and demand a handful of mind-pulverizing barbituates. My Venetian blinds are open. I lean my forehead against the thick, unmovable glass window. Across the court-yard are two windows still yellow with electric light. Rather than giving me solace or slight hope, as they have in the past, they fill me with fresh, damp fear.

◆　◆　◆

A very rough morning. Something wrong with the ven-tilation system and instead of the usual perfect-plus temperature control, an acrid vapor snaked lazily through the bright aluminum vents on my chamber ceil-ing and I awoke to the odor of rotten meat. Or perhaps it was burning rubber. I'm not sure, the olfactory memory is the most fallible. My eyelids flew open and my eyes floated in their almond-shaped orbits, stinging and wet. My eyes did not drift without purpose — in fact, I never do anything without purpose. They were, my eyes that is, still looking for the concealed camera, some ground-glass peeping Tom. I went so far in my belief that I was at that moment being spied upon that I thought the eyes in my favorite painting — a lovely and remarkably restrained Van Gogh portrait of a youth in a blue hat — were not the eyes Vincent had painted but were the peering, obscene orbs of some NESTER flunky, that the spy had snipped the original eyes away and was standing behind the portrait checking me out. Me. And my every move. The notion was absurd but not so easy to dismiss. I thought I noticed a slight shifting of the eyes. Perhaps a blink. I leaped out of bed, made a few meaningless gestures of diversion, like stretching my arms, touching my toes once, twice — groan — a third time, running in place for something less that thirty seconds. Then unable to further subdue my suspicions, I raced over to the painting and placed my finger tips on the eyes. Those blue, kind, canvas eyes. Not the furious gray jellies I had expected to poke. Those indelible eyes. And oh, how I wish I knew that boy, with his blue hat and wispy mustache. That neutral, interesting boy. How I wish I had even one friend in the world. Sorry, folks.

I walked away from the painting, momentarily relieved. Then, with little warning, I became that hideously hidden, relentless recording camera and, seeing myself in the third person, I laughed inwardly at my antics. What's he going to do next, I asked about myself. Calmed by the distance afforded by irony, I breathed a little easier and asked myself again: What's next? Is he going to fall to his knees and start hunting again for microscopic microphones? I had to laugh at this. And continued to laugh as I fell to my knees and looked for the mike, that wire, that shred of evidence. I hunted around, testing a slight crack in the wall near my desk, jammed my fingers into crannies, crevices, corners, nooks, nicks, everywhere. And thought, with a nostalgic throb, of those long-gone days before I was an important man and a bug was something you tried to kill as you spent languid summer evenings discussing sex and taxes on some bore's front porch. Those fleeting, forgotten evenings, when one could still be reconciled with one's wife, when one's career was not in shambles, and all there was to do was suck peacefully on the lime dragged from the bottom of one's gin and tonic and wonder what was the hour. And oh, that young man with the wispy mustache and canvas eyes and interesting blue hat. I would like to have a hat something like that. And, goddamn it, I'll get one next time we go to Boston. I'll get one exactly like that. Mark my words. I'll drag my cronies through a maze of haberdasheries until I find one. And when our day in town is over I'll be wearing it when the car brings us back to work, wearing it as a symbol of defiance that only I'll understand.

A lime green light over my bed blinked on and off and on and off and on on on, signaling me to my office, where apparently I was wanted.

No need, really, to describe my feelings as I took the elevator down three flights and walked through the endlessly echoing corridor leading to my office. My brain seemed poised between the possibilities of catatonia and epilepsy. I made certain I could account for every hour of the past few days. I don't know what good I thought such information would do me, but there was something calming about so cleverly organizing my immediate past.

After eons of agony I reached my office. I stood before it, breathing deeply, trying to manufacture an occupied look to put across my face. I couldn't hold it so I settled for vaguely curious. I opened the frosted glass door and saw, sitting on the edge of my strange desk, Tom Simon, his face tense and vindictive. As soon as he saw me he

asked, "What time is it?" I looked at my Omega —
brand-new — and told him it was 9:40. "I thought so,"
he said with a courteous smile that tended to emphasize
the insidious rudeness of his question. "For a while
I thought my watch was off." He showed me his Cartier
watch. I must learn how to spend my money. "Well,
don't worry," he quickly added. "I won't mention it to
anyone." He smiled and waited for gratitude to flood
from me. Oh, thank you, Tom, I was tempted to say in
my most caustic and effective manner, I am torrentially
grateful to you. When he saw I was going to say nothing
— in fact, I merely stared at him, the door not yet closed
behind me — he went on to say that I had better watch
it, however. "Most of those guys in management are stick-
lers about punctuality.

"Well, come in, come in," he said with peevish amusement, his open hand extended in my general direction. I
came in. Sat at my desk and pretended to be interested
in some stray papers left from the evening before. He
waited for a moment, sensing, with uncharacteristic generosity, that I had some composure to gather. My eyes
scanned some photostats of intercepted letters. And he
waited. I decided to say nothing. If he has something to
say, I thought, let him say it. No prompting from me.

Weary of my pause, he began. "You know your work
has received a great deal of attention. Believe me. We
may be a big organization but we realize we're only as
good as the individuals working here. Without individual
effort and achievement NESTER wouldn't go this far,"
he said, describing some tiny bit of space with his thumb
and forefinger. My blood began to beat at a slower pace.

60

I had that trustworthy animal sense that this encounter was not a prelude to my ruin. "You in particular are being watched." (Oh-oh.) "Your work is considered to be of outstanding excellence." (Ah.) "Of course I only get this secondhand, since my position doesn't permit me contact with your work." He made a self-deprecatory shrug, which he undoubtedly felt he could afford since he was making more money than I. "But I am told that you can sense instinctively the ways in which your findings can be used practically. In the real world. Half the psychs here have such an unbelievably sterile approach to this business." And here he laughed, assuming that we held the same opinion about absolutely everything. "They send in reports that, well, they're just that. Reports. Lists of numbers, graphs, diagrams. But no creative extra. They leave that to the big shots." Another laugh. For the hell of it, I joined him. "Or the computer," he went on. "Now I'm not knocking the computer. Magic Martha — you guys still call her that? — certainly uses those old facts and figures in the most amazing way. But nothing in this world or the next can replace human effort, the extra ummph, the sudden idea." He pointed to the orange and magenta sign on my north wall, IMAGINATION: THE BIG PLUS.

I was feeling better. I was feeling an absurd and delightful sense of relief that is only possible when your nerves have been stretched to their extreme. I resented the icy terror that had gripped me a few minutes before and, by association, resented Tom Simon for bringing it on. I stared at him contemptuously, which I knew at that point I could get away with. It galled me that a raving mediocrity could have found such an important place in the NESTER structure. And it galled me even more that he saw Mr. Worthington ten times as much as I would, ever. Tom at his best was innocuous. He would blend into your mood like an invisible, odorless cream. I picked up a Bic ball point — damn it, I'm going to invest in some really swell pens, some twenty-five-dollar jobs, monogrammed — and, in the manner of the go-getter I was being taken for, tapped absently with it on my desk top. Causing it to wobble. (Why didn't it wobble when he sat on it, with his one hundred and eighty plus pounds?) "Well, Tom, what brings you here? You know what they say about compliments before coffee . . ." I forced a loud laugh, knowing full well that he'd join me. He'd never be one to wrinkle a rapport.

"Compliments before coffee," he said, laughing. "That's cute. No, I didn't come here to tell you how grand you are. Mr. W. asked that I give you this personally." He took out a long, lime green envelope from the inside pocket of his dark blue blazer (Harvard crest on the breast pocket) and put it in my hand. I dropped it in front of me as if it were radioactive. Then I signed a receipt for it — the cursed dread racing like a demon express through bone canals, causing my hand and everything beneath it to shake. Tom tore off the yellow carbon of the recipt and handed it to me. Then he said good-bye briskly. His role finished, his little show all over. Goodbye, Tom.

I ripped open the communication from Mr. Worthington as soon as Tom closed the door behind him. In fact, the click of the closing door coincided exactly with my first attempts to claw open the envelope. And do you know what? It wasn't bad news at all. There was an American Express money order for one thousand dollars — that's a lot of swell pens, a lot of blue hats. And a note, which I noticed a full minute later. It said: "Please be in my office at 10:00 A.M." No signature. None necessary. I looked at my watch — not the most expensive watch in the world but eminently reliable. 9:48 A.M.

◆ ◆ ◆

By the time I reached Mr. Worthington's office I was once again approaching a state of uncontrollable anxiety. I realize you must be getting weary of me describing my blood pressure, my heartbeats, and all the awful internal feelings by which I am plagued. I will try to stop wrapping every third sentence around my upper arm, stop my prose from taking my pulse, as it were . . .

I checked in with Mr. Worthington's secretary, whom I won't, for the sake of charity, describe further, save to say that she is an obese young woman, the fattest person in NESTER, weighing as much as three pounds per inch. After a brief wait in the outer office I was asked to step in — just as the clock reached 10:00 A.M. — and Mr. Worthington was standing, smiling, his eyes bright, welcoming me, and asking me to sit, be comfortable, have a mint.

"How's it going?" he asked as I popped the mint into my mouth.

Stalling for time I concentrated on the white candy. "Good mint," I said.

"Isn't it? It's a new kind, Belgian. Takes away that

morning staleness from your mouth, doesn't it? A remarkable freshening effect." He put one in his mouth and waited for his question to be answered. He would never repeat himself.

"Well," I said, "I haven't been able to work on some things that have been particularly interesting to me, mostly because of that furniture-and-posture study and the mop-up on the eating behavior experiments."

"Yes. I meant to tell you. Your work on the ventro medium thing was very nice. Snappy. I mean that."

I colored slightly. "Thanks," I said in a voice softened by praise. "That's, ummm, ventro*medial*, by the way."

Mr. W.'s features were blank for a moment. Then he smiled and brought his hands together soundlessly. "I know that," he said. "I know that. But that's not why I called you here." His eyes narrowed. He leaned forward.

"Oh," I said. "I was wondering." I straightened myself in the leather seat and fixed my vacant eyes just below his shoulders, where he prefers us to cast our gaze, according to Tom Simon.

Worthington swung around in his chair. "NESTER is a team," he said. "Not an ordinary team, but an all-star team. It lives as a team and it dies as a team. Eats, sleeps, drinks, plays, laughs, and — yes! — weeps as a team. We are a megabody, infinitely complex and interdependent."

I promised there'd be no more health reports, but you must realize that at this point my palms were dampening, rapid electrical waves of fear were rippling through my dura mater, just skimming my most sensitive centers, and I felt my blood being deprived of oxygen.

"And, if anything would destroy us," he went on, "it would be the dying of this team spirit. As you know,

64

NESTER has her share of enemies. Jealous fools, old-fashioned demagogues, spies, competitors, even an ambassador from a northern European country who somehow learned too much. And who must be taken care of, unfortunately. A scrupulous Dane, you know how boring they can be. Anyhow, we are always being attacked from without. It's so ironic. We are industry's final key to success and government's last chance for real power. Yet they attack us. So stupid. So unutterably stupid. Not that this is the case with the majority of them. Most of them know and deeply respect our work. They pay us, they need us, they come back to us. And they protect us, to an extent. But only to an extent. We cannot be at all open about our presence in this very compound, for instance, because certain congressmen and public-spirited boobs would make a fuss. Oh, how I loathe and detest this secrecy. How I look forward to the day when it is no longer necessary. When we can all lead normal lives, be listed on the New York Stock Exchange, teach, grow. If they'd only let us be." His voice was becoming more and more emotional, and he was clapping and squeezing his hands. He paused and put a hand onto his throat, as if searching for a new tone of voice. He took a half-dissolved mint from his mouth and tossed it into a pewter ashtray in front of him. He began again in a quiet, world-weary voice. "And so we go on. Discovering, daring, redefining. We are very alone and very fragile. Though in three days I will be lunching with the Vice President of the United States. Still, we are alone. I have no illusions. Our friends are fair-weather friends. If ever there were a real crisis they would abandon us.

"With so much pressure from the outside, any pressure

from the inside would be intolerable. If any of our team was guilty of disloyalty it would be — would be, well, very sad." (Think of me, friends. My heart, my brain, the oxygen in my blood.) "That's why I've called you here. Not because we doubt your loyalty — quite to the contrary. But because we doubt the loyalty of one of your colleagues. I won't mince words. His name is Carl Stein; I'm sure you've heard of him. We think he is selling us out. We have put information-gathering devices in his office and living quarters but have gained no real evidence. There is some talk about going straight into his brain but I would like to avoid that, if possible. Perhaps he is as innocent as you or me. This whole thing could conceivably be a huge and ugly misunderstanding. He's been with us since the old days when you thought you were doing a job if you tapped somebody's phone. Before things became so complicated. When one didn't care about custom-made suits and a raise every six months. Yes, Carl has been with us for nearly thirty years. And he has been given great responsibility. It is particularly distressing. I hope you will find that our suspicions are misplaced. But we have reasons to believe. I'm not telling you what to do and I'm not telling you how to do it. But anything you can find out for us will be appreciated. We are putting him at your dinner table. Such changes are common and no suspicions will be excited. In one week, again at ten o'clock, come to this office and tell me what you have found."

◆ ◆ ◆

So far nothing on Carl Stein. The investigation proceeds with difficulty. For several reasons, some having

66

to do with him and others having to do with me. He is very quiet during dinners and more than a little unfriendly. He has consistently refused my invitations. I have suggested he come to my room and play a little chess. I have invited him to play squash with me in the health rooms and take a before-dinner dip in the pool. He is simply not interested. But there are certain ethical blocks that hamper my pursuance of the investigation. I'm the kind of brain thief, you see, who'd rather not even know how and under what nasty circumstances the electrode was first introduced into his subject's brain. I'm a picky kind of brain thief in that way. A hands-clean brain thief.

There are other complications: what if Carl Stein *is* being disloyal — perhaps he is just the friend I need, my ally, my Other. Perhaps Carl Stein wants to expose this monstrous power as much as I do. So I am torn between loyalty to who he *might* be and loyalty to Mr. Worthington, who has trusted me and who, when you get right down to it, is a pretty nice guy.

What's worse, though, what's ten times worse than all that is the suspicion that this whole story about Carl Stein is a ruse, a way of warning me that I'm being watched or, worse yet, a way of entrapping me. What brutal, banal cleverness. Subject A thinks he is testing Subject B when in actuality Subject B is testing Subject A. I am, therefore, taking all precautions, I am becoming a baron of the second thought, a king of the calculated risk. I tread lightly from hour to hour, furious and restrained. They'll never get me. At this very moment, as I write these very words, my mind is occupied with other things, other words. Just in case someone is listening in, peeking in my brain. I don't want them to operate on me.

67

I suppose what whips up the gustiest storms of hysteria in me is knowing that one is not really aware of what has happened to one after the implantation. Let me open my files. Look. My treat.

For Subject #44-9-c it started at nine-thirty one Hartford morning. Her well-to-do neighborhood was not often visited by peddlers and when a young (well he *looked* young) magazine salesman came calling in a Robert Hall blue suit, with his hot eyes and long fingers, his glistening hair and impossibly tight collar (these are facts, friends, not my fevered imagination), and he talked about working his way back to veterinarian school somewhere in New Hampshire, and his voice was soft, and promising, and then, again, there were those eyes, as brown as eyes can ever be, perhaps a bit browner . . . I've lost control of this sentence. She asked him in is what happened. He was selling interesting magazines. Special deals. Bonuses. We have no internal reports on her for this time — she was not yet ours — but we have pictures. Pictures of her, a woman of thirty-eight, in her blue and gold housecoat and spangled slippers, with her long brownish hair tied in a pigtail that swung over her thin, curved back like a pendulum as she nodded and smiled. As she thumbed through the copies of *Redbook*, *Harper's Bazaar*, and *Argosy*, wondering how she could help this gentle young man in his silly blue suit realize his dream. It was ascertained that she was alone. The boy walked to the window and made a signal she didn't notice and . . . well, it was all over for her, in terms of peace and autonomy. The Force Recruiters were down on her like gangbusters. With chloroform, in her case.

One hour later she was returned to her home, no wiser. The Connecticut branch is particularly adept at post-operative reconditioning. She had no memory of the boy or his eyes, of the magazines, nothing. She got up from her couch a few minutes before eleven, scolding herself for being so lazy, for not doing last night's dishes, for missing "The Dick Van Dyke Show." It was pure guesswork on the part of the reconditioners, that bit about "The Dick Van Dyke Show." But it was inspired guesswork, since it turns out that is her favorite daytime television show. It has always been a show I rather enjoyed too.

This Hartford mother of three became ours four months ago. She has given us some valuable clues. We've sold some of her data, for $50,000, to a Democratic congressman who wants to run better in upper-middle-class communities. We have noticed increased irritability on her part but cannot link that with the taps we've had out on her brain — though some theorize that even the undetected little transmitter affects certain "nonintellectual" parts of the brain. (Others, and I try to agree with them, say our detectors don't affect the brain any more than a smile can affect the Atlantic Ocean.) Still, she is none the wiser, and, so far, none the worse. The future is not mine to know. If when they were teaching me everything else, someone had taught me to pray, I would say a prayer for the well-being of Subject #44-9-c. Or would I?

What I'm saying — pull up a chair, lads — is I don't want anything like that to happen to me. It's not only that I don't want my dura mater debauched, my rhinal sulcus raped, but I couldn't stand NOT KNOWING. I don't want to be like the hundreds upon hundreds of

NESTER-ized men, women, and — yes! — children who know nothing of their extracted contribution to progress. But they will know. I've promised you that I won't back out. They will know. When all this becomes public. When you are reading this poor jittery journal as a footnote to an awful moment in history. When all you human-interest fiends and inside-dope addicts are gleaning from me a participant's view on the scandal that rocked the Western world, including Paraguay, where we have affiliates. Including Denver, where we've always been strong. Including Honolulu, Tampa, Toronto, and Dover. Including your own hometown, where it has been revealed that the County Clerk's brain has been our switchboard for years and the reason Mrs. Rogers gained all that weight was that she was a part of one of my experiments. Oh, the lost, ugly years, the sadness of revelations. Robbed dreams. Why can't we keep our brains in as safe a place as we keep our money?

In the meantime I must hold my peace. My own situation is not secure. Picture me: the lonely genius trapped behind pulsating radioactive bars of intrigue and sorrow. I must hold my peace. My own situation is far from a secure one. If it were sixty times more secure than it is I would still be living from minute to minute. As it is, I live from tick to tock.

4

EVENINGS MAY BE SPENT in a variety of pursuits. Television is common, chess is possible, snacking and table tennis are both rather popular. There is the gymnasium, the pool, where competitive water games are often played, as well as your steam and sauna baths. Visiting with assigned social partners is possible theoretically, though it occurs only minimally. Sexing is possible. NESTER is strict but not naive, never prudish. Someone suffering from the mindless misery of sexual tension is not likely to work very creatively — though I realize this is debatable. Nazi sexologists waxed ecstatic, you may recall, over the virtues of retaining the semen and the vital protein energy therein. But at the same time, the Nazi party was virtually a traveling sexual roadshow, so we can dismiss such nonsense as cruel rhetoric, produced for the comfort of castrati.

It is possible to have a sex partner sent to your room. It is deducted from your salary. The cost is quite reasonable and the partners are great fun, all very clean and clever and from good families. Still, as the Boys Upstairs undoubtedly predicted, the use of the partners becomes more and more infrequent. These antiseptic surroundings absorb sexuality, suck it out of your marrow and beam it back into you as ambition and work. This has been true in most cases, but not in mine. My previous life had not been very carnal, and now as I trudge toward my middle years I am, at times, consumed by the thought that I have a lot of catching up to do. So I spend almost two hundred dollars a month on sexing. I realize this sounds shoddy and cheap, but for me tawdriness represents a goal, a wild ambition. Also, I want to stress the fact that the girls are wonderful. I haven't had too much pleasant to say about this place as a whole, so I want to make very sure that that yet to be convened committee of congressmen and clerics won't think I'm painting these girls with the same brush. Not only are they courteous and witty, but, as a group, they are extremely pretty. They make you feel like a brave, war-weary soldier. I dedicate this paragraph to the girls and to high-minded hookers wherever they may be. I'd never be so proud as to shun the back door to love.

Despite a heavy hypothalamic heat that generated itself in a slow undulating throb through my arms, loins, and legs, and despite the fact that I felt tonight it would be Karen, crazy crazy little Karen, who would be sent to me, I decided to spend my evening social period talking with Carl Stein. Again, reason splintered itself upon situation and I didn't know if my decision came out of loyalty to myself and my safe well-being, or whether I was trying to

72

earn the $1000, trying to please Mr. Worthington, or trying to make contact with an ally. As it happened I did none of these.

Since Carl Stein is one of my quartet of assigned companions, it wasn't necessary to clear the visit with the Personnel Coordinator or to call Carl's room in advance of my arrival. As a bit of suburban informality and high-level repression, it is commonly agreed that members of the same social sphere can enter each other's living quarters without so much as knocking, any time of the day or night. Real friendly, like. Real scary. But that aspect, of course, no one mentions.

I walked into Carl's room a little after nine. He was sitting in a yoga position before a tiny Sony television set, his old yet muscular legs fantastically contorted, his features totally enthralled with what was transpiring on the small screen. He wore a green velvet smoking jacket and a huge, yellow bow tie. He made no sign of noticing me as I let myself into his small room — which, I was glad to see, was no nicer than mine despite his superior position and seniority.

The show he was watching was "You Be the Judge." It belongs to the domestic-catharsis genre of television entertainment. Someone from the lower middle class tells of a bit of strife in his or her family, usually involving two opposing points of view. Then a panel of fading celebrities discusses the points involved, casting their votes either for or against the plaintive. The defendant (a sister-in-law, a neighbor, et cetera) sits in an isolated part of the studio and through a split screen we can gauge his or her reactions to what is being said — the grimaces, the

73

smirks, the rolling eyes, the peppy forehead slaps, the sighs of utter exasperation.

If the panel of four can't come to a majority opinion, the moderator — an ex-sportscaster — turns to the studio audience and says, "Well, it's time for the People to speak. Folks: You Be the Judge." And the studio audience howls "Guilty" or chants "Innocent," depending both on the case and their mood. Then the m.c. passes sentence. As I walked in, the show was mounting nicely. The m.c. threw it open to the audience and, in near perfect unison, they cheered, "Guilty, guilty, guilty." The screen split in two, showing on one side the ebullient missis, jumping up and down and clapping her hands. She looked like Hubert Humphrey in drag. On the other side of the screen her husband sank into his chair, running his hand through his thinning brown hair and chewing violently on a pink mass I took to be bubble gum. "All right, Mr. Watkins," the m.c. chortled, "you've heard the verdict. And now . . . It's Judgment Time." The band played a burlesque of the old Dragnet theme. "I sentence you to take Mrs. Watkins" — the camera cut to her — "out to dinner every night this week." The audience laughed and cheered. Someone in the audience shouted, "What about next week?" and his friends howled louder yet. "That's not all, that's not all," the m.c. screamed over the mounting cacophony. A quick cut to Mr. Watkins, stuffing his mouth with three more pieces of bubble gum. Then the camera settled on the dreamy-eyed Mrs. Watkins. The camera stayed there as the m.c. went on. "Not only will you raise Mrs. Watkins' allowance ten dollars a week" — an *oooh* wafted up from the ecstatic spec-

tators and tears popped up in Mrs. Watkins' pale eyes —
"but you are hereby sentenced — are you ready for this,
folks? are you ready for this? — you, Harold Watkins, are
hereby sentenced to spend the rest of the month sleeping on the couch." The studio exploded into applause
and screams. The camera swung quickly toward the audience. People were stomping their feet in the aisles and
toward the left it seemed a minor fight had broken out.
Two young ushers pulled a man and a woman apart.
The m.c.'s voice rose above the swell. "And I don't mean
the couch in the living room. THE ONE IN THE DEN."
Mrs. Watkins was crying, swaying hypnotically in her
seat. A quick cut to the panel of fading celebrities, who
stared impassively into space.

Carl Stein unwound from full lotus, stood up, and
turned off the set. "Madness," he said. "They take a
viable concept and turn it into Loony Toons. Cretins.
Every week I watch this, every week I feel sick. You know,
their ratings are very good. It was my idea, the whole
show. Yes. But not like this. There is no catharsis here.
Only tiresome screaming and laughter. There is no sense.
People are too worked up to listen to the commercials.
Did you know that? Sit down, why don't you. Please be
comfortable. Yes, the ratings go up, but the advertisers
are unhappy. Too much excitement. No one listens to
the commercials."

Carl Stein spoke slowly, with volume, dodging the Ger-
manic diphthongs that, even after almost thirty years in
America, shadowed his speech like a sleuth. I regarded
him. Flaxen hair, high shining forehead with a large vein
that beat out a telegraphy of blood. It suddenly occurred

75

to me that Carl was the only person I knew who wore a bow tie. I looked at his perfectly squared fingernails, the smooth, yellowish hands. I knew I was speaking into a battery of hidden electronic ears. Of this I was certain. I had been told. I wondered what my approach would be. If he *was* trying to expose NESTER, was there any way I could clue him in to my sympathies without killing both of us? Clearly, I had no choice but to act in Mr. Worthington's interests. Not in Carl's, not in mine. Besides, there was no reason to trust Stein. Perhaps he was spying on me. Perhaps he was a Maoist or a Nazi. Or a homosexual, I added, looking again at his bow tie, which was not the kind you clip on but the kind you actually tie.

We bantered back and forth for a couple of hours. I was amazed, and a little hurt, to realize how much more responsibility he had than me. He controlled entire communities. He was given extensive use of two-way transmitters, which meant that not only did he receive neural data but he could create it; he could stimulate or obliterate parts of the brain at his own discretion. Only three people in NESTER had that privilege, he told me, after his fifth glass of peppermint schnapps. Everything he said was pronounced with a pinch of pride. He said he left Germany in 1941, and said it in a way that implied it was *the* year to leave, that to leave Germany in 1940 would have been a sign of hysteria and that to leave in 1942 would have been proof of complicity. He said he had never married, as if his bachelorhood were a grand experiment in the human condition. It became eleven o'clock and he took out a box of crackers covered with sesame seeds, which he did not offer me. After every sentence — Carl Stein is one of those people who gives you the impression he is speaking with punctuation — after every sentence he took two small bites from a round cracker. Clearly he was insane. As it neared eleven-thirty, I despaired of ever getting any information from him. I was having no success directing the conversation. Carl was dominating me completely, implicating me in his most passing thoughts. For a moment I considered the abrupt method. I would look at him with steel in my sockets and say: "The Boys Upstairs suspect you to be a traitor and what do you have to say to that?"

Instead, I began to say small, disloyal things, trying to trap him into agreement. What I actually said could not, by any means, be called treasonous, but there was a drum beat of dissatisfaction beneath my words and if he wished to dance that particular dance he could recognize the rhythm. I made fun of the computer technicians. I mentioned my salary and said I needed more. I told him my desk had a slight wobble. Carl didn't pick up on any of it. He was drinking schnapps and eating, with that mad meticulousness, sesame seed crackers. He was diverting me with his habits, hypnotizing me with his pace. He would take a sip of schnapps, and take two small bites of a cracker. Then he would utter a sentence. Then two more bites of cracker. A pause. Small sip. Sentence. Two small bites of cracker. A pause. Legs crossed. Sentence. Uncrossed. Two small bites of cracker. A sip. How could I get through to him? In desperation I said things I shouldn't have. I felt, even though every word was monitored, Mr. Worthington would understand that what I was saying was strictly in the line of duty. Still, I was indiscreet. I said I sometimes felt sorry for my subjects. He sipped, took two bites, said something completely unrelated to my words. I mentioned my disappointment in not being allowed to witness my funeral. No reaction. I looked at a spot in the wall where I imagined a camera might be and winked at it conspiratorily. Covering all bets, as it were. I said the food we got was boring. I said I would like to try LSD. No reaction. Nothing. Boldly, I took the glass of schnapps from his small, yellowish hands and took a sip, hoping to derail him, to throw a wrench in his ritual. He stared at me impassively, like a panelist on "You Be the Judge." "You know that Miss Mitchell," I said, "the woman who trains the Force Recruiters?"

Slowly he took the glass from my hands. He looked at the glass and then at me. I listened to the purring precision of an electric clock that sat between us on a small table. Carl produced a white handkerchief from his smoking jacket and wiped the rim of the glass where my lips had touched it. The clock purred on. He folded away his handkerchief with intriguing care. Finally, in a rather soft voice, he said, "You are scum, did you know that? You are scum. You have been in my home for hours and nothing but complaining. Why are you here? You are womanish and cowardly. Observe how your hands tremble when I confront you with what you are. History has somehow permitted you to enjoy a place in one of her greatest moments and you can think of nothing but objections. Wobbling desks, poorly seasoned soups. You are an impossible man. Childishly fixated on everything that matters least. I should report you, but I will not. It is not to my liking to indulge in office politics. Besides, you are yourself your own worst enemy." He screwed the cap onto the nearly empty bottle of peppermint schnapps, closed the box of crackers, and stood up. Though he was very angry he showed virtually no emotion. "You will please leave now. It is late and I am in need of rest. I have much to do and we are not friends."

I attempted to say something but could find no words. I slowly got up and made my way to the door. He quickly walked across the room and opened the door for me. "You are truly scum," he repeated. By now his voice was showing the strain. He was quivering around the vowels. "I dislike you with such intensity it is necessary for me to strike you." And as I attempted to walk past him and out into the hall, he punched me in the shoulder blade with all of his might.

I staggered back to my room and immediately tore off my shirt so I could see the damage that had been done. There it was! A bruise. In the center of my pink back, a boysenberry badge.

◆　◆　◆

I stopped my morning's work today about a quarter to twelve. I was hungry and somewhere, somehow through NESTER's antiseptic hush I smelled curried shrimp from the cafeteria. I was damn hungry. Hungrier than I could remember being for months. So hungry, in fact, that I wondered if some hideous hypothalamic stimulator-depressor wasn't busily at work, lousing up my limbic system. Certainly the thought of the tables

79

turning was a constant one. More so since the night with Carl Stein. How easy it had become to imagine my unconscious being piped into the insatiable electronic jowls of the computer downstairs, mercilessly masticated and belched up as some sure-fire sales approach, or a way to marshal opinion in favor of some new and insane government project.

These were my thoughts as I hastily stacked some stray papers and prepared to leave for lunch. The feeling of hunger was, however, so pleasant, so human that I dismissed my fears and prepared to go to the cafeteria. Carl Stein and I were no longer eating together. He had apparently requested a transfer after our evening together and the Boys Upstairs, acknowledging my total ineffectiveness as a sleuth, readily complied. So I was looking forward to a pleasant lunch, and as I left my cubicle I felt positively happy.

I closed the door to my office, searched vainly for my reflection in the frosted glass window, turned around, and was met by Tom Simon's vaguely unpleasant stare. We looked at each other for some short period of time and then old trusty Tom looked at his watch. Trusty Tom's trusty watch told him, naturally, that I was leaving a little early for lunch and he checked it a second time with a mock sense of justice. "It's lucky I caught you," he said. He paused here, waiting for me to agree that, yes, it was lucky he caught me.

Instead I said, "What do you want me for?"

"*I* don't want you for anything," he answered with a chill. "Mr. Worthington, however, wants to see you in his office." Then, pausing cruelly, he stared at his watch again. "Well, let's be going. I'll walk with you."

I stared at him, uncomprehending. Had I come this far in life only to be led from room to room, regardless of my wishes? What was it about the world that every day you seemed to have less freedom, less choice? And what if I didn't want to go to Mr. Worthington's office? And what if what if what if? What had happened to all my what-ifs?

The long walk. With Tom Simon silently beside me, checking his watch and looking . . . expectant. (Think of my hands, my feet, the beating of my blood.) The endlessly echoing corridors. Where was everyone? Where were my fellow employees? Why this silence? Hello? Hello? Before long we reached Mr. Worthington's office. Tom paused impressively before the door, which was embossed with a huge W. God, I thought to myself as I regarded the enormous initial, that's class. That's for me. We stood there, Tom and I, united for a moment by a shared awe, a nascent greed, as if a garden of forbidden delights awaited us. Didn't we know? Couldn't we remember? It would only be Mr. Worthington, in the office with the green rug. And he'd be sitting there. Of course, his desk is enormous, and there's an array of telephones, Dictaphones, recorders, buzzers, the screen of a closed-circuit television built right into his desk. But on the debit side, his hair is dull gray and he would be sucking a mint. He would offer us a mint. Perhaps he wouldn't offer Tom a mint. But me, certainly he would offer one to me. Was there anything in this man to be afraid of?

My first surprise on entering the office was that it was in a state of total disarray. Lined along the walls were various pictures and plaques that had been taken down

81

(a black, brown, gray, and white oil painting of turn-of-the-century factory workers walking through a snowstorm was my favorite). There were pale rectangles on the walls where the pictures had once hung. Boxes filled with books — the bookcases empty. Some of the telephones were disconnected and stray wires lay across the floor like faults in the earth.

Mr. Worthington himself seemed to be in an uncharacteristic state of agitation. He was opening then closing then opening again a drawer in his desk, shuffling violently through a stack of onion-skin papers that made fragile, helpless sounds as he pawed them. The outer office and waiting room, where his rotund secretary had once resided, had vanished. Her desk was gone, as if it had been traded in for the patch of bare floor that now took its place. The wall that once separated her nook from his domain had been knocked down or slid away and the office looked immense and unsafe. And Mr. W. looked smaller, angrier, apt to do something rash. Tom and I swayed deferentially, standing as far back as we could, waiting to be noticed.

He found what he had been looking for, apparently, for he withdrew a piece of paper from the drawer, made a small satisfied sound, and shook his head bewilderedly. He looked at the paper quickly and ripped it into tiny pieces, dropping the confettied information into a lucite wastepaper basket. Then he looked up and nodded at us and we stepped forward. "Thank you for bringing him, Tom," he said, as if I were some inanimate object that had been delivered.

"Will that be all, Mr. Worthington?" asked Tom.

"That it will, Tom," answered Mr. Worthington in such a way that I sensed some bit of feud between them. Two of the phones on his desk began to ring. He picked them up and hung them up in one motion.

Tom left and I was comfortably seated in a high-backed pigskin chair, offered a mint, and, since nothing had been said yet, given sufficient time to dread my fate. My first fearsome thoughts were very general, having to do with a vague feeling of persecution rather than a sense of being punished for anything specific. I had a brief run of pain fantasies, thinking of the most excruciating tortures. Then regret, the old familiar, Why did I get into this in the first place? I began to wonder what exactly I was wanted for at this moment.

Mr. Worthington was leaning back in his soft leather chair, swirling in a 45-degree arc. Then: an abrupt stop and his body veered forward, his elbows propped suddenly on the desk. "You didn't meet with any great success regarding the matter of Carl Stein. I realize it was a difficult assignment. Not really your lie — pardon me, not really your line. We had hoped that your effect on Mr. Stein would be more neutral. I am afraid we did not envision you as such a controversial friend. Oh, do try and smile. There is nothing so bad in all of this. You tried. We know that. How is your back? It was a nasty sock he delivered, we understand."

I shifted my weight, as if the mention of my bruise had somehow activated it. As a matter of fact, I had forgotten about my back. Being in Mr. Worthington's office made me think more of other parts of my body: my heart, my bowels, my jugular vein. "Oh, it was nothing. Line of duty and all that. Ha ha ha." I wondered why Mr. Worthington's never laughed at any of my jokes. Why he never even did the old broad-smile-and-head-shaking routine that is possible when a laugh can't be forced. Inflexible bastard. I loathe people who put such a premium on being "authentic." Or was it that he was recalling my treasonous words in Carl's room?

"However," he continued archly, "we have not been without success in the matter of the good Mr. Stein." He chuckled lowly, a barely audible eek of amusement. "No, not without certain very real rewards for our concern. Are you interested in hearing how our little melodrama concludes?"

I stared at him, not really understanding this was my cue. After a bewildering three quarters of a minute had dragged by, I said, "Yes."

"Well, it seems that Carl, Mr. Stein, was using our scientific information for most unscientific purposes." He paused reflectively and, noticing my mouth had stopped making those small sucking motions, offered me another mint. "Yes, Carl was one of the originals, as I may have told you. An excruciatingly brilliant man. Who knows? Perhaps the most brilliant man working here."

I felt a twinge of jealousy.

"His passing will be a great loss to NESTER — though there are those who insist he had outstayed his welcome. A brilliant man — why do you frown when I say that? You were not impressed with him? Oh, at any rate, who is to say what is brilliance? Carl Stein turned out to be, after all, a petty larcenist — and a bungling one at that. But in the field of information gathering, extrapolating, and projection — the best. Among the younger people in the field there are more very good ones but fewer, far fewer of the greats."

There was a knock on the door. Mr. Worthington's pale, placid eyes turned upward in exasperation, profoundly expressing his obvious annoyance — he was just getting into it. "Yes," he said, deliberately stripping the word of any quizzical intonations. The door opened slowly and Ira Robinson peeked in, as if he were an emissary from a different dimension.

"You asked to see me?" he inquired, still unwilling to enter the office.

"Yes, I asked to see you," replied a weary Mr. W., "but I said one o'clock. You're early."

"Oh." A pause. Ira was in inexplicable agony over the innocent mistake. "I'm sorry. My secretary said as soon as possible."

"Your secretary was in error."

"Oh. I *am* sorry."

Then with an unexpected flourish of generosity, Mr. Worthington conceded, "Or perhaps *my* secretary was in error. It has been known to happen. As you see, things are rather unsettled here. But be that as it may, it is not time for our meeting. If you would be so kind as to be patient and keep yourself available, I'll buzz your office in a few minutes."

The usual ruffled moments passed in the wake of Ira's departure. Then Mr. W. continued, "Yes. While a few minutes are still available to us, let's conclude the sad and miserable tale of one Carl Stein. As you know, Carl had perhaps more power than any nonadministrative person in this entire organization. He had been with us for a long, long time." Mr. W. paused and a soft mist passed slowly over his gray eyes as he remembered, no doubt, the good old days, when a brain thief was a brain thief. "For years Carl had been initiating projects — most of them charged with his special genius. K-eleven-six-b was his, from start to finish. All of our latent hostility projects came from him. He was, among other things, a master of anxiety. A dip in a chart, a squiggle on an EEG and — poof — Carl would have a product. He was, for instance, the father of feminine hygiene.

"Now, looking back over his career, I hold myself somewhat responsible for his going wrong. I trusted him perhaps too completely, was too easily carried away by his infectious enthusiasms. Carl would come to me with a plan, a new approach, and I could never say no. If it was a question of money I would have the budget budged. Equipment — no problem. Helpers? Fine. He had only to mention his needs and I would make quite certain they were satisfied. And believe me, my faith and trust in him helped NESTER become what it is today. Most of the people here, we have found, work better when closely supervised — too much freedom frightens them, depresses them. Yet Carl was different. He was the master of the modern slogan, a poster poet. Make Love Not War was his. As was Register Communists Not Guns. Was there anything he could not do? If one criticism were to be leveled, it would be that his ideas were too fresh, too ahead of the times. For instance, he would invent a slogan and it would sometimes take six months for it to catch on. And even though all of us knew that eventually it

86

would be on the tip of the national tongue, the waiting produced its own anxiety. Clients would be nervous beyond description. Black Power, for instance. That took years and years to really catch fire. Carl was a little psychic, I should say. In some ways it was merely a matter of experience, of course. A matter of knowing that A and B most often led to C. But with Carl one couldn't help feeling there was something else involved, some mysterious machinery of genius."

There was another knock at the door. Three sharp raps, almost authoritative, causing Mr. Worthington and me to start in our seats. Without waiting for word from Mr. W., the door flew open and three NESTER maintenance men came in, in their dusty-blue NESTER jumpsuits, so attractive really. "We came for the rest of it," announced the one with the darkest hair, and they began to stack cartons in each other's arms. They moved swiftly and silently, as if auditioning to be Force Recruiters. They took books, file cabinets, paintings. Their agility and strength were impressive and I was glad to watch them for a while, suffering from moral vertigo as I was. Carl Stein, Carl Stein, the name clattered in my head like a castanet. I stared at the workingmen. Why do the stupid seem less doomed? And I stared at those dusty-blue jumpsuits — I hate to tell you this, but they were periwinkle. Periwinkle! With that brilliant embroidery on the sleeves. The N . . . the E . . . the S . . . Someday all of us will be wearing them. The way we dress now is so impractical, so unsuited for . . . jumping. They left the office with some difficulty, arms overloaded, struggling to get through the door. As they made their way out,

I noticed that the dark-haired one, who, because of the one sentence he spoke I took to be the leader, was wearing a small hairpiece near the back of his head and that this extremely dark brown toupee had somehow slipped to the side, making him look quite ridiculous. He also must have sensed his hair was askew. While still in the doorway he supported his load between his chest and the wall and with one free hand deftly straightened his wig. His two companions laughed immoderately. One of them closed the outer door with his foot. Slam.

Mr. Worthington leaned back in his chair, evidently under some strain, and closed his eyes. He pulled a box of chocolate mints from his jacket pocket and popped two in his mouth, rudely forgetting to offer me one. Then he snapped forward, as if miraculously regenerated. "Well, you should be happy. Your potential importance here has increased. Of course, we all have potentials. But your potential is now potentially greater." He laughed, perhaps maliciously, perhaps ironically, conceivably out of nervousness. The phone jingled meekly and he lifted it and dropped it in one easy motion.

"We suspected Carl Stein of disloyalty. We were right. We hated to see him go. Perhaps it was partly my fault. None of us, certainly, none of us who gave him so much power — we were none of us blameless in the matter. It could have been worse, however. It could have been much worse. You see, he was not really traitorous, he was merely greedy. That was all there was to it. Warped and acquisitive. There was nothing" — Mr. W. shrugged and extended his lower lip — ". . . political. Nothing like that. He was merely making commercial contacts on his own, on the outside."

88

Without even knowing I was going to speak, I blurted out, "Why? Miss Dorfman — my bloody secretary — can go out; Carl Stein, that violent crook, can go out. But I can't. Is it fair? I've been meaning to ask you. Why some and not others? Pardon the interruption, but it's important to know. I long for a subway ride. I've never gone fishing. I'd like to try that sometime. I feel cramped. It's not fair that some should and others shouldn't."

Mr. Worthington looked at me and let me know in a painfully silent way that I had overstepped my limits. He spoke evenly, patiently, hopelessly, as if he were explaining combustion engines to a duck. "It was necessary for Carl Stein to be outside at certain times. Not necessary for his soul, but necessary for his work. Just as it is necessary for me to spend a certain amount of time away from this installation. I don't think really you should question such things. Your future here is incredibly bright. What lies in store for you can only be guessed and hinted at. Please, for all of our sakes, don't throw it away out of petulance. Don't throw it away, don't don't throw it away."

"I won't," I promised, believing for that moment my humble vow.

Mr. Worthington smiled at me and quickly glanced at his watch. "We'd better hurry this on," he said. "This is a busy day. Let's consider the Carl Stein case closed. Have you deposited that one-thousand-dollar money order in your account yet?" I told him I had. "Hmmm. Well, we should withdraw it. It was payment in advance for a job on which you were virtually useless. No offense. But that particular assignment could find no point of contingency with your particular talents." Mr. W. sighed

89

and looked at me with an almost fatherly smile. "But it is so tiresome to withdraw money once it is cozily ensconced in one's little nest. Let's see . . . why don't you return a couple hundred this afternoon — give it to Mr. Delaney in bookkeeping — and keep the rest as payment for good intentions. That was a nasty bruise he inflicted on you. Yes. That is, I think, an equitable decision."

As I became more accustomed to speaking with Mr. Worthington, I grew more adept at recognizing the cues he would glide my way. It was somewhat the familiarity lovers are reported to feel. The partner arches his back: the young lady strokes it. The young lady closes her eyes: the partner kisses her forehead. Yes, I was becoming attuned to Mr. W., closely attuned. The pauses were less awesome, the ellipses less elusive. So I knew what my question was supposed to be and I asked it. "Just what was it that Carl Stein was doing, if I may ask?"

"He had gone into business for himself. He was investing in various firms and then pumping the firm's message into his subjects. He was no longer banking with us. Numbered Swiss accounts. Very sordid. One simple example will suffice. He had thrown in with an independent electrical power company. The most ruthless kinds of capital-lusts." We had a brief but enjoyable laugh, Mr. W. and me. "Name of the firm was Southwest Independent Power Company. A young, rather attractive firm run out of Arizona. We sent somebody out there to check on it. Our most pessimistic theories proved true. He had not only been acting as a consultant but he had been doing a fantastic neuron-to-neuron promotion job for them as well. NESTER had given him considerable clout out there in Cowboy Land, as he used to call it, the bastard. People were, quite naturally, clay pigeons for his incessant prodding. I mean, it was the crudest thing imaginable. It wasn't bad enough that he was selling Southwest information; no, that wasn't enough. It wasn't bad enough that he gave them a scientific basis for a regional campaign — and a brilliant campaign at that. No, he didn't stop there. He must have been insane. Truly mad. He actually began to send messages to his subjects. 'Switch to the Southwest Independent Power Company,' he would tell his subjects. 'Switch now, tell your friends.' How many people could he influence that way? Fifty? Two hundred? A thousand? What was the point? A penny-ante mentality. He must have been out of his mind. What else could it have been?"

"That night in his room," I said, "when he punched me. Even before that. He was eating seeded crackers and drinking schnapps. I thought he was insane."

"Did you." Mr. Worthington cast a cold and humiliating glance my way. How quickly people change. How few friends a divorced man really has. And then, as abruptly as he froze, he melted. "Well, I'm glad that it's over and glad there are people like you with NESTER, dedicated and brilliant men, forward-looking, selfless, and shrewd. It is a bad day for Mr. Stein and a good day for you and, let us pray, a good day for all of us." Mr. Worthington stood up and stretched. He yawned voluptuously; his pale gray eyes went all milky. "We had better call it a day. I have several meetings today and you must be absolutely famished. If you hurry down to the cafeteria you can perhaps get some curried shrimp — I be-

91

lieve that's what they're serving today." He leaned over his desk and wrote something on a note pad, tore the top piece from the pack, and handed it to me. "And if you are too late to eat there, then call this number and lunch will be brought to your office. This has been a good talk, hasn't it? I think we are becoming quite attuned to one another. That's important. And if your future in NESTER is to be what we all think it will be, it will grow more and more important. If not crucial." He offered me his spotted hand and I shook it tenderly and said good-bye.

As I walked toward the outer door I once again noticed the remainder of the picture frames, file cabinets, and cardboard boxes that were strewn about. I turned around to question Mr. W., who was already on the telephone. "What's happening?" I asked, waving my hand over the clutter.

He looked up at me, startled to see I had not yet left. He put his hand over the receiver and whispered loudly. "I'm changing offices. This place gives me the creeps."

◆　◆　◆

I walked directly back to my office, opened the door, and saw Mr. Worthington sitting at my desk, his old hands folded in front of him. "How did you get here?" I blurted.

He smiled slightly and directed me to sit down with the merest flickering of his eyes. "I want to ask you a question," he said.

I have built a barrier between consciousness and hysteria and my thoughts flew against that flimsy screen like a thousand suicidal June bugs. For example: Did a secret passage connect my office to Mr. W.'s? Had a

92

chunk of time been embezzled from me? I figured maybe 90 seconds had separated my departure from Mr. W.'s office and my entrance to my own, but perhaps an hour or two had passed, miserable, mute minutes during which I had been subjected to untold, inexorable indignities. Or maybe Mr. W. was some kind of sensational sprinter. "What is it?" I finally asked.

"Do you like working here? Is this what you wanted?" He stood up and wrung his long white hands. He moved past me and stood briefly at the door. His back was to me now and he waited for a moment while I struggled for a reply. Then he was gone.

5

I TOOK THE REST of that day off and slept for sixteen hours. I had eleven dreams and I remember each one vividly. I was up at 7:30 A.M. and took a long shower, shifting the temperature of the water from hot to cold to hot again. Marvelous. A long leisurely shave, still naked. I turned to see if the bruises had faded from the middle of my back. Yes, gone. As mysteriously as Carl himself.

I thought about what shirt I would wear, what tie. This successfully occupied me for an hour as I tried every shirt and tie combination in my wardrobe — which is quite meager and only serves to remind me that I must get to Boston soon and spend some of this fabulous money I'm making. I finally settled on an ultramoody dark royal blue shirt and a parochial-school green tie. Somber yet threatening, I thought. I also wore a nicely cut herringbone-tweed jacket and black pants. To show that I was serious but not depressed I put on my brown Hush Puppies. Nudity as a life-style would never do for me. I look so

94

much better with clothes on. I appraised myself approvingly in the mirror and, just for the fun, leaned over impulsively and gave my reflection a little kiss on the nose.

There must have been a time lapse or something. Something must have sneaked up on and startled 8:30 and caused it to jump all the way to 9:20, because all of a sudden the lime green light above my bed was blinking on and off telling me that not only was I late for work but someone was waiting for me in my office. Jesus.

I ran down the two flights of stairs, zipped through the ever-echoing corridor, and was in my office in less than two minutes. To no one's surprise, Tom "Mock Justice" Simon was waiting for me. I closed the door behind me and leaned on it as I tried to catch my breath. Tom watched me huff and puff and then, in a mournful voice, asked me, "Why are you so hostile to the schedules we've set for you?"

"I'm . . . I'm . . ." — still winded, you see — "I'm not hos — hostile. I'm just late. Two" — swallowing hard; a lump of something had risen in my throat — "two different things, Tommy."

"You are always late."

"That's not true and it's not your business."

"It is and it is."

"Not and not," I intoned, showing my big teeth as I spoke.

He was evidently taken with this. He rose from his perch on the corner of my poor, weakened desk and sat on the couch. He lighted a mentholated cigarette and sucked in deeply. "Where is Mr. Worthington?" he asked me.

"How should I know?" I growled, still ready for the kill.

95

"I repeat. Where is Mr. Worthington?"

I became concerned. "Is he missing?"

"Missing? Did you expect him to be? Have you heard or seen anything that would suggest such an eventuality?"

"No."

"Yet you suspect something foul has happened to him."

"I suspect absolutely nothing of the sort. You came in here and asked me where Mr. Worthington was."

"First of all, it was *you* who came in here. I was already here. I was waiting for you. Secondly, I didn't ask you where Mr. Worthington was. I asked you if you knew where he was."

"Tom," I said, "you are a complete asshole."

Tom heaved a long, disgusted sigh. Mock Justice made way for Mock Suffering. "Let's start from the top. Do you know where Mr. Worthington is?"

"No."

"What would you do if it were imperative to see him?"

"I would ring his number."

"And if it's been changed?"

"I'd call personnel."

"And if it's unlisted?"

"I'd ask around."

"Oh, that would be bright. That would be absolutely brillant. That would be in strict accordance with security precautions."

"All right, Tom. I have no idea what I'd do. I'd probably just shoot myself."

Tom looked startled for an instant and then heaved another suffering sigh. Well, Mr. Worthington has asked that I show you to his new office. You'd better take a jacket. There's still a draft."

96

We took an elevator down to the ground floor and then a special elevator into the basement, where the computer and the computer programmers and the computer technicians live. We came to an immense, windowless, lime green door. Tom put a card, which bore his picture, into the aluminum-colored slot and, after a buzz of recognition, the door opened to us. "Do you have one of these?" Tom asked, showing me his card. He knew I didn't. I told him of course I did. He snorted at my lie. We hated each other.

We walked past two dozen scarcely partitioned officettes. Programmers were busy with the precious personality print-outs created by folks like me. I stopped to look at a young, extremely striking Korean boy who was sitting immobile at his desk, a salmon-colored rubber ball in his slender hand, squeezing and unsqueezing, staring straight ahead, immersed in the abstractions of the day. Around the chrome base of his swivel chair were three yellow pencils, broken in perfect halves. Tom was staring at me, hands on hips, furious at the moment's delay.

We came to the room that houses the giant computer, Magic Martha. A huge concoction of whirling reels and flashing lights. It was half as long as a city bus and ten feet high. Looking at her reminded me of how closely related are our concepts of time and our understanding of human limitations. Our smallest unit of time is the second — we just don't do things faster than that. For Magic Martha a second is a long long time. Last time I asked, she was making most of her decisions in a nanosecond (which is one billionth of a second) and many of them in a picosecond (one trillionth of a second). Since then, I am told, she has become much more efficient.

There were about fifteen computer technicians wearing lime green smocks hovering around MM, feeding her, consulting her, listening very attentively to her every beep and squeak. It seemed that not one of them had ever spoken a word to anyone, so completely did the ceaselessly spewing machine occupy their every moment.

Tom and I continued our little stroll. Past a few smaller computers, a row of memory banks, and into the computer workers' cafeteria, where they were preparing turkey noodle soup. At the far end of the cafeteria we came to another immense lime green door which Tom again opened by gratifying the electronic device with his identification card. It opened up to a wall of elevators, each one initialed with a different letter. There was a P, a McG, a S, a B, and a few others. The W was on the far left and was freshly painted. As soon as Tom pressed the sparkling white doors the elevator opened up and we entered it. Inside, the elevator was carpeted with fur and lined with mirrors, except for the north wall which was covered with lights that snapped on and off. These lights, I was later to learn, took our picture and filed it permanently, searched our person for concealed objects, and got a general idea of our state of health.

In less than a minute the elevator opened up again and we walked out to a dark brown tunnel and the whistling of high winds. There was a small yellow and black car — not a car, really, for it ran on tracks and the tracks led to God knows where. It was not shaped like a normal vehicle. It was a thin yet sturdy-looking yellow metal bar that adhered to the tracks by two grooved wheels.

On either end of the bar were two black cubes, hollowed out. Since it was too noisy (from the howling wind) to speak, Tom motioned me into one of the cubes. He was trying to be abrupt and officious but it was apparent that he was terrified — he had only made this trip a couple of times and he was far from used to it. Both of us settled into our seats and, God knows how, the vehicle whizzed down the darkening path.

I loved it. Though I was frightened and cold, it seemed jaunty and unusual and it gave me what they call in the trade a heightened sense of life. "Yippee," I screamed against my better judgment. Marvelous, I thought. At that moment of exaltation I wanted to be very good friends with Mr. W. and visit him often.

Too soon, the Krazy Kar glided to a stop. Tom was shivering stoically, staring into space. I jumped out of my compartment and rubbed my hands together. "Well, Tommy, what next?" This end of the tunnel was bright and warm and as I asked Tom the question I noticed Mr. Worthington's obese secretary waddling toward us.

"Coffee, gentlemen?" she offered uninvitingly as she whisked us into a small waiting room, separated from the tracks by a sliding glass door, which reminded me of the little rooms where you pay your fee in public garages. We sat on a crescent-shaped couch which encircled half the room. Very comfortable. Tom, sensing my pleasure, glared at me and began thumbing through *Modern Photography*. I, as I am wont, leaned back and considered my fate. It was, I remembered, May 20. In fifteen days I would be thirty-five. I was getting better and better at my work. Respect was coming to me. I had taken a ride on a rapid underground car. I had been recently punched. I was a brain thief.

I looked through the glass wall and saw Mr. Worthington with his arm around Ira Robinson and they were both laughing wildly. He walked Ira to the yellow and black car and, as Ira entered the hollowed cube on the left, they shook hands. Simultaneously they touched their finger tips to their chests, where the heart is. In a moment Ira was gone. Mr. Worthington turned and saw us in the waiting room and waved enthusiastically, even going so far as to stand on tiptoe.

Mr. W. disappeared as unexpectedly as he had appeared, and his secretary came into the room and asked that we follow her to Mr. Worthington's office. We followed her down a short hallway lined with flashing lights and up to a very ordinary-looking door with frosted glass, much like the one in my office. She opened it for us and we walked in.

I must admit that I was a trifle disappointed with his new office, especially after the incredible journey. Except for its immensity and the beautiful silver bowls holding assorted mints (Ceylonese mints, ginger mints, Junior Mints), it was a perfectly ordinary office without a view. There were pictures resting against the wall, waiting to be hung. The bookcases were half-filled and several cardboard boxes full of books were stacked near Mr. W.'s huge, black Formica desk. He *did* have a fur rug, however. Wall to wall. And there *were* eight video screens built into the wall behind his desk. The wall, by the way, was gray plastic — very smart. Also built into the wall were a bar and several lamps that looked like motorcycle headlights. On second thought, Mr. W.'s new office was pretty damn nice. I could feel the fur rug right through my rubber-soled Hush Puppies.

"Thank you, Tom Simon, for braving the journey and bringing our friend to me," began Mr. Worthington in an exceptionally good-natured voice. Then, looking at me: "Tom isn't much on our new arrangements. Ha ha. But that's the price you pay when your boss gets a big promotion." He leaned back in the black leather chair behind his desk and popped a mint into his mouth. He was feeling great. "The car should be back now, Tom. Why don't you take this time to attend to those matters we discussed last night." They traded significant glances and Tom quietly disappeared.

Mr. W. got up from behind his desk, stretched his old arms — the slowness of his movements sadly emphasized how far along in years he really was — came over to where I was uncomfortably standing, and pounded me heartily on the back. "Well," he said, "what was it you wanted to see me about?"

I colored quickly, feeling very vulnerable. "You sent for — me," I finally managed to say.

"Joke. I was just joking. Ha ha ha. I know I sent for you." He looked at me as if I were crazy. Then changing moods with his usual nonchalance, he clasped his hands behind his back and said, "I feel marvelous. Simply one hundred per cent. I called you down here, first of all, so you'd know where I am if ever you need me or want to shoot the breeze. This door, my friend, is never closed to you. Don't think this promotion business is going to make me forget any of you up there. I don't care if all my new and important administrative duties have to wait until midnight for my attention, I think you boys in science are where the action is and my first responsibility is to you." He put his old spotted hand on my shoulder. "And your first responsibility is, of course, to me."

Mr. W.'s secretary came in with two plates of scrambled eggs and Canadian bacon and two cups of coffee. There was a rectilinear lucite table set unobtrusively to one side of the office, where we sat down and enjoyed our breakfast. He talked with his mouth full. "You know," he said, demanding my attention with a wave of his fork, "I sometimes think there is precious little connection between the life I'm fortunate enough to lead with NESTER and the life that I led before coming here. In a way, my life has been a double feature." He laughed and, momentarily embarrassed, washed the egg down with a lusty swig of coffee. "I'm more than sixty years old, did you know that? How old did you think I was? Come on. Be honest."

"Early fifties," I lied.

He looked disappointed. "Really? A lot of people figure me for forty-five, forty-six." A pause. He looked troubled. "Anyhow. Don't you think this is a great new office? And that underground track." He described a speeding car with his hand through the air. "Zooooom. Do you know what I am now?"

"A speeding car?"

"No, no." He looked at me again as if I were crazy, a slower, more searching stare. Then he burst into laughter, reaching across our breakfasts and patting me gruffly on the cheek. "You're fantastic. I meant do you know what my title is. I'm a first vice president now. Quite a jump from senior unit supervisor, don't you think?"

He went on like this for about fifteen minutes. How we were such pals. How lucky he was. How someday perhaps I'd be in his place. How there was no one *presently* in NESTER whose abilities he admired as much as mine. How good the eggs were. How he hoped his secretary — Miss Andrews —never lost an ounce. Really, he said virtually anything that came into his head. It was nice to see him so relaxed, though I couldn't help but think that his mind was wandering. What was most annoying, however, was to realize he would be talking on and on like that no matter who was with him. He was just in the mood, that was all. He wasn't really talking to me. I just happened to be a pair of available ears. *That* hurt.

Perhaps Mr. W. sensed my restlessness, for, as he sopped up his eggs with a piece of whole-wheat bread, he said, "You know, Paul, I think you are very wonderful."

Again I colored. Mr. Worthington often reduces my responses to those of a teenybopper. "Me?" I said. "Wonderful?"

"Yes, really," he said, nodding sagely. "You have taken so splendidly to your work here. Your production has been superb — you were, I think, born for the work. And never a peep of complaint. This may be a little shocking to you, but we often have a messy time with our workers, especially during their first few months. But not you! You just got right down to work and you've been plugging away ever since." He sighed. "I want to do something for you," he said. "I want to show you you are appreciated."

"Perhaps I'll be able to leave the compound," I suggested.

"You are not permitted your day in Boston?" he asked, concerned.

"Oh, yes. But I was thinking that perhaps I'd be able to go in on my own. At night, maybe. Whenever I wanted."

Mr. W. smiled. He was a civic-minded old man playing Santa Claus at the orphanage Christmas party, listening to the poignant, impossible dreams of the abandoned children. He chuckled. "Now let's not get into a hassle about *that*," he advised, his voice hardening. "All right?"

"All right," I said.

"But there *is* something we *can* do for you, friend," he continued in a more relaxed tone. "How about if we gave you a few of our special subjects to work on? How does that sound?" He leaned close to me. "How about a few of our X-rated subjects? Ordinarily, we require at least five years' seniority before we give our people access to sexing experiments. But I am willing to look the other way if you're interested. Some of it's pretty strong stuff. And what you'll be required to do is of a breathtakingly sophisticated nature." He sopped up the last of the egg and poked the bread into his mouth. "You interested?" he asked.

I nodded.

"What? Can't hear you."

"Yes," I said. "I'm interested."

Mr. Worthington jumped from his chair and exploded with laughter. "I thought you'd be."

Sensing my interview was over, I got up. Mr. W. held me tightly at my upper arm and led me to the door. "We'll be sending you data — films, EKGs, and some tape recordings — presently," he said.

"Thank you," I murmured. (Perhaps at that moment I should have smashed him in the face, destroyed his office, and produced a submachine gun to shoot my way out.)

"You know," he said, "there's a little something I'd like you to do for me. I've been pretty free in letting you 'do your own thing' and I'd like you to do this for me. I want you to pay a visit to one of our guests here, a top employee and someone I want you to meet. There'll be no punching, I promise you. When you speak with him, observe him and gather your impressions. I want you to drop me a memo or — if you'd like — come to speak to me about him. His name is Leon Anderson. Now, be careful. We have a *Len* Anderson here, but we've got him working in the cafeteria. I'm not awfully interested in your seeing *him*." Mr. W. smiled gaily and gave my arm a squeeze. "But I think it's important that you see Leon Anderson, who's a real communications sharpie. First rate. All right? Can I count on you?"

◆ ◆ ◆

On the way back to my office, I heard a prolonged burst of maniacal laughter. I was standing not far from my office, in the bleak green corridor surrounded on either side by closed office doors with frosted glass windows that

105

seemed to regard me like so many encrusted, dead eyes. I whirled around but couldn't determine where the sounds were coming from. I waited for the doors to open, for curious, intelligent faces to peer into the hall, for modulated inquiries. But no door opened, no door cracked, and then the laughter stopped. I shrugged and continued toward my office, walking slightly more slowly.

A shot rang out — a violent crunch of ragged black noise. I felt as if I'd been kicked in the center of my heart. My bones shook and hummed like railroad tracks over which a howling diesel had just passed. Overlapping the last reverberations of the gunshot was a deep, swooning groan. Then there was the sound of a body slumping over a (kidney-shaped?) desk, a gun escaping from a lifeless hand and falling to the floor, and finally a human form, now lifeless, rolling slowly through the stages that separate humankind from corpsedom and ending up on the floor.

By now I was whirling in circles, my eyes flashing, my jaw working. I wasn't certain from behind which door the fatal shot had cracked. None of the twenty or so doors opened so it could not be figured out by a process of elimination. Finally, after what seemed like several months, three Force Recruiters came padding down the hall in their thick-soled shoes. Following them was a scrawny young doctor in a white suit and white shoes. He looked terrified. They went to the office two to the left of mine and opened the door. The hulking heavies peered into the office, looked at one another, and nodded. The doctor tried to fight his way past them and finally he did. I was at this point pressed against the wall, hoping

106

not to be noticed. There was, of course, no chance of this. I mean, I am wearing this suit and tie, my hair tends to be curly, and I am the only person in the long, sterile corridor, the only person at all, and of course they see me immediately. But they seemed not to care. The doctor fought his way out of the office and said, "Dead." The Force Recruiters rushed into the office and picked up the corpse. Holding it by the feet and the head, they ran down the hall so fast that I couldn't determine if the victim was someone I knew.

♦ ♦ ♦

I staggered back to my office and tried to immerse myself in my work with the same fond, foolish hopes a decrepit codger carries into the painful, sulphurous swirls of a mineral bath. Gingerly yet determinedly, piece by piece, deep into the steaming yellow water — someone, somewhere, said that it was good for you.

First I sat down and tried to read an article in one of the more respected journals of physiological psychology that I authored while still an academician. It was called "Hippocampal Neuron Responses to Selective Activation of Recurrent Collaterals of Hippocampofugal Axons." I stared at the title. As I remember it, I had called the article "The Hippocampal Neuron Responses . . ." but some jerk at the editorial desk had deleted my definite article. This filled me with quiet, aimless rage. I skimmed through my article. It was not remarkable. Much of it was filled with the results of other people's experiments. There were four passing, rather snide references to colleagues which, upon consideration, I found humiliating. It was, I think, the first piece that had ever appeared in that journal to use the word "incredible." Yet, for all this, there was something poignant and bittersweet about it. Its mediocrity had a brave and heartbreaking quality. It was not the work of one who was storming the frontiers of the unknown, but it was not the work of a goddamned brain thief either.

I remembered writing the final draft. My adopted son had just convinced me to buy him a walkie-talkie and I had felt compelled, for purely financial reasons, to do my own typing. I remembered sitting in my minuscule study, pounding out the paragraphs, mapping out the charts, sipping Hiram Walker from a jelly glass, cursing the paucity of my destiny. Why couldn't I have been contented with that tiny frame house, that stormy marriage, that adopted son? Surely there were people less significant than I. Academics and run-of-the-mill scientists, it suddenly occurred to me, have pleasant old ages. There are pensions, retirement plans, honorary positions. Does NESTER have a retirement plan? I had worked until dawn on that piece — thirty-one impeccably typed pages. Then I fell asleep in my chair — not because I was too exhausted to trudge up to my bed but because I had always wanted to be discovered at my desk, papers in front of me, my head thrown back, my mouth open. Maybe it was from a movie or from some other more private dream. I awoke the next morning about 10:00. The house was empty. My son was in school and my wife had gone ice skating in an indoor rink with her half-sister. My neck was stiff. Lydia! Why didn't you awaken me with a glass of juice and the morning paper? Friends, family, why didn't you peek into my study and let the sight of me melt your hearts?

I threw the magazine onto the floor and lowered my head onto my arms. My desk wobbled as if in seizure. I looked up, my eyes red and blinking. I wondered if that chap's suicide was going to be prominent in my dreams. This compound is a terrible place for nightmares. After a distressing dream it is crucial to have a warm body to press against, even if that body no longer loves you. After a nightmare it is helpful to get out of bed, go to the kitchen, and eat that last piece of broiled chicken. But in NESTER there is nothing to do after a horror dream except open your eyes and regard the walls which seem to be regarding you with unusual interest. From the darkness behind you, eternity seems to be breathing on your neck.

I am no stranger to these dreams; they spring from my pontine fibers at will — their will. Often my experimental subjects stumble toward me in my dreams. They hulk my way, their skulls insectified by clumsy electrodes, their jaws working up and down, their fingers wiggling in my direction. You used me for room-deodorizer experiments, one chants. Another with sullen, empty eyes points to her swollen middle, mutely accusing me for my part in eating behavior experiments. Still another accuses me of disseminating addictive drugs. And one young man throws a specially designed easy chair in my direction — a prop in my gamma neuron studies.

But who wants to hear about my dreams? Even the innocent have nightmares. Even the pure of heart wake up in a fright, clutching at the clammy sheets. What dif-

109

ference does it make if one faint-hearted brain thief finds his sleep patterns disrupted by his compulsive, macabre visions? I can't expect pity. I can scarcely expect patience. I know, I know. This is not news to me. I am not well-liked, nor will I be for some time to come.

I'd like to change jobs. Unfortunately, for my peace of mind, this makes it necessary for me to blow the lid off the most blithely sinister organization in the Western world.

I'd like to change jobs and it may cost me my life. I want my unemployment checks sent to northern Europe, to Denmark. My mistress will pick them up for me at the post office and then she'll come back and we'll make love and then have soup and then we will continue her English lessons. I am teaching her "weather words." Cloud, rain, umbrella, lightning . . . Look how she gazes at me — the respect, the compassion. I am a hero. Perhaps we won't make love. It doesn't really matter. The nights are cold. I am having trouble sleeping, still. She is rocking me to sleep. Perfume rises from her breasts. Soon I must leave. A vast underground railway. Interviews in the avant-garde press. They are still on my trail. They want me dead. I told the world. Perhaps we won't have soup. In the morning we look out the window and see there is blood in the snow. Someone has killed all of our goats.

I've had it. I've really had it. I don't want to work here any longer. I'm not on NESTER's side. I am not loyal. I don't want to live like this. I have bad dreams about my subjects — they come to me empty-eyed and groping. Accusing me. I told you that. I could have helped them, they say. I didn't. I played along. I helped ruin the world. The world is ruined. That is hard to believe. Perhaps it is they, my victims, and not my captors who will catch up with me in Denmark and murder our goats. Oh, the future. The future makes me tense. This is no way to live. I've got to get out of this.

6

JUST FIFTEEN MINUTES AGO I staggered back from Leon Anderson's room. The visit was a favor I was supposed to do for Mr. Worthington days ago, but I've been too busy. All my life I've wanted to be busy, to have pressing engagements, to be up to my neck in something crucial. For instance, when I was on the outside I always envied men who were too occupied to answer the telephone. Even a simple thing like calling my insurance agent and having his secretary tell me that he was "in conference" would fill me with sadness and envy. I was always the sort of man who would lunge for the phone on the first ring, hoping it was something major. Now I am a truly busy man, an involved man, and even a favor for Mr. W. must wait its turn.

Unlike the Carl Stein mission, this visit to Leon Anderson promised no financial rewards for me. Maybe I was still working for the original $1000. An annoying prospect since, if my memory serves me right, Mr. Worthington deducted a couple hundred of that fee because I more

112

or less failed. I must remember to inquire about my financial position. I am losing track of the details of my life . . .

Thanks to another from-the-top decision from the personnel department, Leon Anderson was put on my visiting cycle and I was free to stop in and see him at any time. (Visits to anyone not on your official cycle are, of course, forbidden.) When I entered his room he didn't seem at all surprised to see me. (I know if someone just popped into my room I would be, well, very surprised.) "Who are you?" he asked me. I introduced myself and he nodded quickly as I spoke. His room was essentially the same as mine, except there were no windows at all and there was complete disarray. His bed was unmade, clothes hung out of half-opened dresser drawers, little balls of tightly squeezed tissue paper lay in an indecipherable pattern across the room, and everywhere, everywhere there were telephones. Telephones and tape recorders. There must have been at least thirty telephones and six tape recorders. As I let myself in, Leon was holding a telephone to either ear while a tape recorder made electronic noises of varying pitch. Aside from the telephones and tape recorders, there were mysterious yellow boxes, three of them, with tiny red needles that quivered over crescent-shaped gauges. And folders and folders of computer print-outs.

"I just felt like stopping in," I said. "I had no idea you were busy. Why don't I come in some other time?"

"Hogwash," said Leon with a genuinely friendly smile. "I'm always busy. But never have been too busy to visit with a friend. No sir, I've never been that busy."

He was a small man and he wore a brown-and-green-checkered sports jacket and green slacks. His glasses were too large for his face and his watch too small for his wrist. He had sandy hair which he wore in a crew cut and there was a little dotted line of perspiration above his lip, as if that were the place one was supposed to rip his head in two. He shook my hand with depressing effusiveness; I regarded him with an unmistakable distaste.

I had no idea what Mr. Worthington wanted me to discover about Mr. Anderson, other than his rodentlike loathsomeness, which was immediately apparent. Was Leon also suspected of disloyalty to the lofty ideals of NESTER? If so, I would have gladly exposed him, since I had no wish to strike an alliance or even come to a gentleman's agreement with him. Or was I merely supposed to check him out, see how he was doing with his projects, judge him as a human being in some semifinal way? Or perhaps it was part two of Mr. Worthington's trap to catch me making some treasonous statement. That possibility depressed me no end. Not that I wasn't guilty of disloyalty that would undoubtedly far exceed his most malignant suspicions. No, I was guilty, all right. But how could Mr. W. think I was so stupid? He was dealing with a master of deceit and he was treating me like a fool.

Anyhow, since I didn't know what was expected of me, I decided to make my visit brief and play it by ear. I looked for a place to sit and, finding none, edged myself onto a corner of Anderson's bed. "How long have you been here, Leon?" I asked him, deliberately using his Christian name.

"I don't know," he said with his abrasive twang, "are we supposed to tell people that? I don't think so. I don't think we're supposed to tell people that."

114

"I've been here for a year," I said very casually.

"Oh, really? I don't know if you're supposed to tell people that." He began to fidget with the telephones around him, moving them this way and that. He picked up some needle-nosed pliers, looked at them, and then put them down again.

"You're never at any of the meetings for the psychologists," I said. "At least I've never seen you."

"You know why that is?" he asked with a slight smirk.

"No, why?"

"Because I'm not a psychologist." He laughed uproariously at this, going so far as to whip off his glasses and rub his left eye.

"Oh." I was beginning to feel uneasy. I felt my chest, half-expecting some cruel cardiovascular prank. "What do you do, then?" I asked, determined to keep sanity in the conversation for as long as possible.

He looked at me suspiciously, running his small brown hands over several phones, as if he expected them to answer my question without his permission. "I'm a communications expert," he finally said after tremendous delay. He looked at me, hoping he had satisfied my curiosity. I just stared back at him blankly. "Communications," he repeated with a shrug, gesturing at the shiny black barrage of telephones that surrounded him.

My eyes made their way around the walls of his room, wondering where were the peekaboo cameras, the hidden mikes. It was my usual routine, something I've come to do automatically whenever entering an area of unexplored space. If Mr. W. went to the trouble of suggesting I visit Leon Anderson, then the chances were this was being monitored and I wanted to do well. I decided to put him a little more at ease. "Where you from, Leon?"

He thought for a moment, either trying to remember where he was born or trying to decide if he was allowed to tell the people that. "Oklahoma," he answered with a smile, confident that he had done the right thing.

"Oklahoma, huh. I had a sister-in-law that lived in Tulsa. Are you from around there?"

"Let's just say that I'm from Oklahoma."

I pushed back his rumpled green blanket and made a little more space for myself on the edge of the bed. I tried another approach. "You know, Leon, I fully appreciate your concern for security in these matters. Believe me, I'm one person who can understand that. Yet I think there are limits. After all, we're all on the same team, we're all aiming our shots at the same mark, and I think it's important that professionals in the same field take the same time to discuss their work. Especially if they're working on different aspects of the same problem. You're in communications. Now, you might not believe this, but I'm not even certain what that means. Do you follow me? Right now, I'm doing work on the ventromedial nucleus of the lateral hypothalamus and I've done some pretty classy things with the gamma motor neuron."

Leon nodded eagerly as I spoke. He seemed terrifically interested in everything I said, an exasperating response but one that softened my attitude toward him. "You're a psychologist, right?" he responded.

"That's right." I nodded. "And you're in communications." I had decided to treat him as a lunatic. "Isn't it great to be here? I mean, to have an opportunity to participate in all of these wonderful projects. This is un-

116

doubtedly the most advanced center for this kind of work in the whole world and it's a great honor for any professional man to be here. Don't you agree?" I shot a glance toward where I had decided the camera was hidden.

"Oh yes, you bet it is," Leon chimed. "Yes sir."

"Then you like it here?"

"Like it here?" Leon whipped off his glasses. "Hell's bells, this is a dream come true for me. I've got everything . . ." His voice suddenly trailed off and he put his glasses back on. He picked up his pliers again and picked a half moon of dirt from beneath his thumbnail. "I don't know if I'm supposed to say this," he said softly, "but I've only been here a couple of months. Before that I was working about fifty miles outside Oklahoma City. I was working at this place . . . well, it's a long story. It was kind of a telephone and radio outfit. Nothing fancy. We just made parts mostly. I was an engineer there, you know. And I'd be screwing these transistors into these mounts and all day long my head would be popping — just popping — with ideas. I mean, let's face it. You got a product that goes into every home in the world. Right? O.K., you take that product and you monkey around with it this way and that and if you know what the hell you're doing pretty soon you got yourself a situation where you can influence all those people that are using your product."

"That's right, Leon," I said. "I'm learning how to do that with foods."

"Foods? Well, that's great. Foods." He whipped off his glasses. "Foods? You put something in their foods, right? Like something that makes them want to screw all the time. That's great." Glasses replaced. "Well, right

117

now I'm working on the dial tone. You follow me?" He picked up the phone that rested against his knee. "Every time you pick up a phone you hear a dial tone. A clear signal. Why should we waste it? Every day, millions and millions of people hear that sound. That is the most listened to noise there is, if you're talking about a noise that's the same every time. Now, some of you boys down in psychology have been doing some checking on this and there's no doubt that certain pitches of sound can make the brain do certain things. Like dull a pain, or make your ticker beat quicker. Well, I want to take it a step or two further. I want to put a very subtle sound through this phone and I want that sound to make whoever hears it feel so afraid he won't want to go out of the house. I'm not going to be stupid about it. I don't plan to have him feel the fear as soon as he hears the clear signal. That would be dumb. It'll be a slow-acting thing. And it'll build up over a period of months. They won't know what hit them."

"You mean the whole world's going to be hiding beneath their couches?"

"No, not the whole world. At least *I'm* not going to be." He smiled. "But some one person or group of persons will certainly be in a lot of trouble. I'm not going to say who but I think you know what I mean. This thing can be controlled. Certainly our friends aren't going to be using phones like these."

"Well, how's it coming?"

"It's coming, it's coming. Just a matter of working out the details — and you know how hard that is sometimes. Hard as picking an eel out of a bucket of snot. But I've

118

been thinking on this little idea for quite some time, and now that I'm here I can just completely devote myself to it."

"That's great," I said.

"You bet it is. It's what I've always wanted. It's a dream come true. I can't hardly tell you how badly I wanted this." He paused and stared at me with a scary intensity. "I prayed for something like this," he rasped.

"Really?"

"On hands and knees. Through many a long and lonely night."

"Lonely?"

"Lonely as a fish on a cactus."

"Mmmm."

"Hard times."

"I'll bet," I said.

"I took to playing crazy games with myself." His voice was getting furry. "They ain't secret. The people in charge know about them. I took to pretending that people were following me. I played at being hunted. I committed the newspapers to memory and then put them in a paper shredder I purchased at considerable personal expense."

"I don't understand."

"Well, looking back on it, I see I was pretending to be reading, you know, secret documents."

"Oh."

"Seem familiar?"

"No. Why do you ask?"

"Just a habit. Whenever I get to talking about myself I always ask that question."

119

"What other games did you play with yourself?"

He drummed his small fingers on top of one of his telephones. He dragged his tongue over his teeth. He took a deep breath, as if at that moment he expected the room to fill with water. "Games?" he asked, exhaling and raising his thin beige eyebrows.

I made a rolling, please-continue gesture with my hand. "You were saying . . . ?"

"I wasn't saying shit," Anderson mumbled. "I mean if my problems don't even sound the least bit familiar to you."

"No, I wasn't saying that . . ."

"Then you admit it!" he said, coming back to life.

"I really don't know what to say."

"We all of us have pasts. Faint, moist mosaics that make us what we are." He paused. "Do you know who said that?"

"No."

"A man who works here. Name of Worthington. Do you know him?"

"No," I lied. "I don't think so."

"He's top-drawer. Gives me everything I want. I don't know that he'd understand what I'm up to but he supplies the materials and gives me the time."

"Sounds all right."

"I already told you," he said slowly, "it's a dream come true."

7

IT'S BEEN DAYS since you've heard from me. I wish I could tell you that in this time I have planned my escape from and exposure of this place or I have made contact with an ally here and together we are cooking up some succulent scheme . . . but in fact I've been quite alone and my thoughts have been steamy and inward. I have been, that is, acquainting myself with some data for Mr. W.'s promised sex experiments. The work is driving me into a deep, voluptuous sorrow. NESTER takes things for granted that, in my previous life, I used to relegate to the realm of remote, fantastic delights. We are, for example, comparing alpha deltas for anal intercourse, oral intercourse, and multiple sex. (We have detected a brief period of spindling that the three have in common and can already shift brain patterns to stimulate — in a perfectly chaste situation! — sexual responses until now associated with congresses of profound immorality.)

I have been reading the files, checking the charts, perusing the print-outs, and it is driving me mad. My own sexual fantasies have been so . . . lame. For instance, I have always dreamed of walking alone through a spacious public park and coming upon a thin, dark-haired girl in a raincoat who is sitting on a bench and sobbing softly. The exotic thrill that that fantasy holds is *I ask her no questions,* but only sit next to her, take her hand in mine, and press my lips fervently onto her palm. She looks at me with the world's sorrows in her eyes and I take her deep into the woods and undress her. Then we make love. Such is the meager heat and cunning of my own erotic imagination.

Even as a married man, my sexing was self-conscious and infrequent. Lydia always claimed that I physically neglected her, but there was a look in her eyes when I got into bed that told me she did not want me to touch her.

Today I was permitted to view some data extracted by the reality condensers (film crew). The movies are supposed to bring us into closer, more intimate contact with our subjects, though they have never affected me so. The cast of characters changes too quickly; subjects are here today and gone tomorrow. In the time we have with subjects we get to know them pretty damn well, obviously. But intimacy? Never. We mull over a lime green folder filled with charts, watch perhaps a few thousand feet of tightly edited film, correlate our data, figure out a pattern, and if possible make a few tentative remarks. But is this love or even friendship? Once a project is over the subject becomes invisible to us once again. True enough, he is perpetually wired and forever ready to go, but ninety-nine times out of one hundred you never see or hear him again. He is integrated into a new experiment and some other equally fickle doctor is recording the beeps and blips of the subject's secret self. The subject's brain is treated as a whore whom we all abuse in turn.

Ah, but the films! The films! They are delivered to my office in dark brown film cans girdled by a black canvas belt. They are labeled with code numbers which correspond to files of data. Such a batch was waiting for me when I came in this morning, and upon finding them my mouth went dry. These were the first I'd seen. I sat at my desk, routinely considering my fate and drumming my fingers on the film cans. I pressed a triangular plastic button near my telephone and a humming filled the slowly darkening cubicle as black curtains were drawn over the small window with sinister slowness and a projector slithered into sight from behind a wall panel. Then I stood on a straight-backed chair and, tiptoeing tensely, hooked my pinky into a copper ring with which I pulled the sparkling white screen down from its metal cocoon near the ceiling.

Upstairs, at this very moment, Miss Mitchell was putting the Force Recruiters through their paces. Clatter clatter bang. They must be a new batch. Heaven help me . . .

I had planned here several pulsating paragraphs describing the fleshy shenanigans represented in the films, but looking through the notes I kept while watching them I see that they were, in a sense, like the first moon shot (and all of the subsequent thrusts toward that piece of dead rock) — more exciting in conception than in actuality. When we thought about our sweet boys adrift in those rockets and aloft on the moon our blood quickened, but when they were actually there, dragging themselves about and trying to remember the things they had been coached to say, it was all we could do to keep our eyes open and more than a few of us wished that the telecast would be interrupted by an urgent message from "My Three Sons." So it is with pornography. Although I have never attended a pornographic movie, I am certain the most arousing part of the experience is after the purchase of the ticket when you are standing alone in the pink and black lobby, checking your reflection in the smoky mirror. Once you are actually confronted by the bodies in all their imperfect nakedness, heaving at each other, grimacing and grunting, going at it with all the poignancy and grace of tractors, exposing their genitals to the smooth glassy camera — it is true, classic, quintessential boredom. Perhaps there is an inverse relationship between the psychic power of a conception and that concept's resonance in the physical world. Yes. The more interesting and moving a thing is to think about, the less interesting it is actually to see, for instance juggling or socialism.

For hours I watched the films. Our subjects are mostly white and middle class. Some of them looked strangely familiar. There were more than fifteen consecutive minutes of various men lifting the black nighties of various women. Up/Cut/Up/Cut/Up/Cut. Tummies and tits and some hands so hairy that they looked gloved. What were these films supposed to prove? My head rolled, my eyes glazed, yet my attention remained with the films as if attached to their banalities by a steel thread.

There was one particular rounded, gently fuzzed belly that looked like Lydia's.

A shot of a woman's buttocks. The cheeks are grabbed

124

by a pair of strong, masculine hands. They are kneaded and then forced apart. The screen momentarily darkens as he brings his body close to hers. There is no sound. Then, like a third party, the man's erect penis approaches the woman's backside. A clock is superimposed over the image. As he inserts himself into her the second hand begins to move. Then superimposed on the lower left-hand corner are twin grids representing the subjects' EEGs and in the lower right are similar grids representing their EKGs. They are heaving and grinding, the second hand is sweeping, EEG and EKG lines are scrunching, leveling, peaking, falling, flattening, and leaping, and I am virtually in shock from the whole thing. Perhaps it is all stimuli for a test they are running on me.

I kept at it until I fell asleep at my desk. Then I gathered up some folders (my neck was a little stiff from dozing in my chair) and brought them to my room, where I looked at them until midnight.

◆ ◆ ◆

Some years ago, in the middle of a brutal winter, my wife and I gave an open-house party to celebrate our first anniversary. By the time it was ten o'clock, it was obvious no one was going to attend our little affair, save the three or four life-long friends who were already there, picking their ways through the cold cuts and drinking heavily. Lydia, I remember, gave me a long accusing stare and then burst into tears. She was biting on her fist, mumbling all sorts of vilifications — oh, it was awful. She has always been a denouncer — and I the denounced — but that night she outdid herself. Even God was on the carpet, Hat in Hand.

I hustled our guests out, literally shoving their over-coats into their arms and sweeping them out onto our front porch, where, for all I cared, they could spend the rest of the evening. Lydia was still in tears when I returned — if anything, she had gotten worse. Careful not to disturb her, I began collecting all the plates of virtually untouched food. I emptied the mixed nuts into their original can. The Hershey's Kisses found their home in a plastic bag. The plates of cheeses and crackers were covered with plastic wrap and put in the refrigerator. The cream cheese and celery concoction, the dainty Norwegian flatbread, the assorted Swiss chocolates — I wrapped them all very carefully. Then the long, delicately arranged plates of salami, ham, roast beef, and turkey. It was necessary to wrap the different meats separately. I used tin foil, making a boatlike compartment for each cold meat and then sealing it tightly. In half an hour it was impossible to tell that the house had once been prepared for a night of festivities.

I sat next to Lydia, who was curled into our corduroy couch, still sobbing. I ran the tip of my finger over the bristling fuzz on the back of her neck and then, in one easy motion, squeezed her shoulders, with both of my hands. She cringed and shook her head violently. So I went to bed. I undressed slowly, took a sedative, and read something tedious as I lay in bed. The sounds of her crying filled the house.

◆　◆　◆

They are really piling it on. Lackeys invade my office with a ceaseless flow of new information — new films, new print-outs, small cassettes in pearl gray plastic that contain warbles, sighs, and moans, and manila envelopes filled with 3-by-5 black-and-white snapshots. There are pictures of women naked and alone in bed, men on toilets, strangers on a train. There is a teen-age girl in shiny black boots and a flimsy white T-shirt — nothing else. There is a picture of a woman mounted on a man and two small boys seated at the foot of the bed gazing at them forlornly. There is a picture of a man in a business suit turning around and staring at a young woman who has fallen down on a city sidewalk and exposed one ponderous thigh. This male was Subject #312-s-15. I looked at the picture for quite some time.

It is the theory of the Boys Upstairs — I don't know why I call them that, my Boy Upstairs is in the basement — that studying stills supplies us with certain information that we can't get from the motion pictures. First of all, there is the physical thing, the fact that holding a picture in your hand helps you focus your attention on it. Then there is the portability factor. A snapshot can be looked at anywhere, any time, whereas looking at movies is a minor technical ordeal. But the most important benefit of the stills is that they demand an involvement from a brain thief, an involvement that perhaps your average brain thief is not accustomed to. The snap extracts his imagination. We are pretty spoiled here. Stereoscopic, stereotaxic, stereophonic data are readily available to us. Results are neatly tabled, categorized, and computerized. Our research *can* become mechanistic. With the photographs, we must work for our clues. The snaps are merely moments, however cleverly snatched, from an alien, unsuspecting life-span, and it is up to us to make sense of them.

Upstairs now, the Force Recruiters kick down the doors in perfect unison. Miss M. has whipped them into shape in no time.

I no longer have the slightest interest in sleeping with her.

I am staring at the pictures.

I am staring at my hands.

I am wanting a life of my own.

◆　◆　◆

On a piece of yellow paper with light green lines I am keeping a list of names and addresses of NESTER victims whose files have passed over my desk. I keep the paper — no, I won't say where. Perhaps at any moment a fury of Force Recruiters will come kicking into my room to arrest or demolish me. Why should I tell them anything? Let them tear this place up looking for the things I've hidden.

Assuming, however, that I *do* make my way out of here — a plan has not presented itself to me as yet — I will find these NESTER-ized people. I will travel through the Dakotas or up to Vancouver or down into Alabama, wherever my victims reside, and I will put it to them: You have been used as a subject in a ruthless, illegal experiment. I will probably get punched. I will probably be laughed at. I will sit on a train and cross the names off my list one at a time. I will meet someone on the train who will fall in love with me.

For I realize, finally, that more will be expected of me. It will not be enough, after all, to testify before that congressional subcommittee. Screaming the facts over all the airwaves is likewise insufficient. I must help undo what has been done.

How helpless and alike we are. I have never in my life been moved by human frailty but now the mere thought of it — our delicacy, our foolishness, the shortness of our lives — brings tears to my eyes. I have taken to crying myself to sleep and thinking about God.

When I was eight years old I detected a certain impossibleness in the story of Noah and the Ark and began calling myself an atheist. When classmates asked me what religion I was (there was in my school a fierce Protestant-Catholic competition) I would say I was an atheist and often I would get pushed down. I would come home sooty and torn and my mother would ask me what had happened. I would tell her I'd been shoved about for my unpopular beliefs and she would stare at me with faint horror, for she knew this meant I had trumpeted my atheism outside her house, something I'd half promised never to do. "Well, what do you expect?" she would say, biting her lip and turning away.

Grief stamps about in my heart like a petulant child. My loneliness can find no object to fixate itself upon; my sorrow can find no subject upon which to dwell. Prisoners of war, I imagine, can fall asleep with tearful visions of homes and families undulating in their consciousness. Mother, father, the wife, the kids, the old backyard, the pool hall, buddies. Prisoners in federal penitentiaries stare at wrinkled photographs of loved ones, fantasize about times past and things to come. But I have nothing. There are Lydia and Andrew, no more real to me than shadows in the water. I think of Andrew in Forest Hills with the walkie-talkie I bought for him . . . nothing. I think of the soft fuzz on the back of Lydia's neck and I stare at the tips of my fingers, scarcely able to believe there was ever any contact between the two — that fuzz, these finger tips.

If I were to bust out of here right this moment, where would I go? I try to imagine myself in Lydia's mother's apartment building in Forest Hills, the Grover Cleveland. I am standing in the elevator, lurching toward the fifteenth floor, staring at myself in the small round mirror that is somehow supposed to stop crime in elevators. I am padding down the narrow, bright hall, then rapping on the door. They let me in. (I have already been announced by the surly doorman.) Lydia is wearing a flowered, quilted robe and furry slippers. She has been under the sun lamp and her nose is red. "I'm back," I say. "I'm alive." Lydia's mother comes in, an old lady with blue hair and small wet eyes. She is carrying Andrew in her arms. He is wearing pj's with a cowboy and Indian pattern on them. He has a cast on his arm. The cast is autographed by his new friends. He is far too big to be carried about. His feet are dragging on the floor. He obviously recognizes me but he considers my presence some kind of threat. I am standing there, hat in hand, sweating like a pig, consumed by the mistaken idea that if I could only think of something witty to say everything would be a lot better. "I was a brain thief and I wish to repent," I blurt out. Lydia's mom drops the kid and races toward the telephone. She wants to have me arrested for impersonating the dead.

8

I TOOK SUPPER ALONE in the cafeteria this evening. My tablemates, Freddy McCarthy, who is in pharmacology, and Irwin Glass, who is a psychiatrist, had recently departed, leaving in their wake a barely sampled cherry parfait and a small bit of apple brown Betty. I put these aside and started on my tomato rice soup, my creamy coleslaw, and my grapefruit juice. As I was finishing this three-part prelude to sliced turkey, Tom Simon sat down at my table. He was grinning so wildly I thought his usually rigid face would crack. The strips of overhead light blinked in my silver fork as I turned it over in my hand. "Hello, Tom," I said. "You get transferred to this table?"

"No, I just wanted to tell you that I've been kicked upstairs."

"Oh?" I said, not really understanding.

"Yup. I'll be occupying Mr. Worthington's old office. It's fantastic. I mean, I never expected it."

It was my turn to speak but my throat was slowly closing.

"Anyhow," Tom continued, "I wanted you to know, since I'll be supervising you in certain ways. Now you understand" — and here he reached over and gave my arm a small squeeze, causing me to lose half a forkful of coleslaw — "you understand that I'm not a scientist. My duties are administrative. I make things work." He locked the fingers of both hands. "I make the gears mesh." He noticed I was staring malevolently at his hands and he dropped them to his sides. "Anyhow," he went on, "my only wish is to make your work easier, more pleasant, and, of course, more fruitful. You'll have to bear with me these first couple weeks," he said with a small laugh that told me this was the sixth or seventh time he had delivered this speech verbatim. "I've got a thousand little details to tend to, and, frankly, it'll take a while for me to hit my stride. During that time I would suspect that I'll often be calling on you and your associates for assistance. My only wish is to make your work easier, more pleasant, and of course — of course we will all of us do our best to make this administrative transition as smooth as possible. I want you to feel free to drop into my office at any time. And I will be paying you many unexpected visits." Here he paused, waiting for that veiled threat to undress itself in my mind. "Anyhow, it's going to be interesting. As you can imagine, I'm a little beside myself with excitement. I feel deeply honored to be promoted to this position. And I will do everything in my power to show myself worthy of NESTER and worthy of —"

"Tom," I said with a wave of my hand. "Please."

A brief silence. Tom stood up. He reached into his pocket and pulled out a roll of candy. "Care for a mint?"

132

he asked. Shocked beyond belief, I took one. Tom said good-bye and walked away. I stared at the circular white mint that sat in the palm of my hand. Who was he kidding? Tom was striding jauntily toward the cafeteria exit. I closed my hand over the mint and then, without really thinking, I threw it at Tom. It was a pretty good toss, though it did not hit him. It skipped a few inches away from his feet and then shattered. He stopped in his tracks and looked at the pieces. Then he turned around and looked at me. I stared fearlessly in his general direction.

♦ ♦ ♦

Later that day in my office I ran some recently acquired films from the sexing experiments. I sat behind my desk and watched the luridly flickering screen with one eye and doodled absently on a pad of yellow paper. Hearing of Simon's promotion had put me into a deep funk. A series of montages materialized. I watched. Suddenly impotent men having their heads cradled by their unfulfilled mates floated before me. There were shots of the horrified males biting back tears of rage and shame and close-ups of the women. Some women seemed really annoyed, some frightened and guilty, some faintly amused, but most surprisingly calm and compassionate, an attitude which, according to the requirements of this particular study, is not experimentally significant but which rather surprised me and raised my opinion of women two or three percentage points.

It was Friday. At the end of every week each employee must submit a brief report of whatever he is working on and, if available, a synopsis of his findings. We are given lime green folders in which we are required to clip six or seven pages of reports and they are usually collected in the late afternoon. I had had mine ready since Thursday evening and the shiny green folder sat on the front of my desk with my name and the date inked onto a piece of white tape at the bottom left-hand corner. At about four o'clock a tall man with gray hair and a skimpy blue sports jacket entered obsequiously and flashing what is known as a "shit-eating grin" grabbed my weekly reports and tucked them beneath his arm, where he carried a couple dozen identical green folders. "Afternoon, sir," he said, turning away. He opened the door and I saw his aluminum pushcart in the hall, stacked high with folders as well as unbound manuscripts, print-outs, and long yellow writing pads.

I had always assumed that my reports were sent directly to Mr. Worthington, who thus kept tabs on me and my work. I wondered if this new batch was being carted to Tom Simon — a depressing, sickening thought, as disturbing to me at that moment as hearing that a piece of emotional poetry I had written had fallen into the hands of an enemy who read it aloud at a party to which I was not invited. That was something, by the way, that actually happened to me back in high school, though I don't bring it up with the hope of excusing any of my subsequent behavior. Suddenly I had to know if my reports were delivered to Worthington or Simon.

I opened my door and peered down the corridor. There at the far eastern end was the tall old man with his pushcart. He was waiting for the elevator and I raced down

134

the hall to catch him, leaving the projector running. (When I returned, the film had run its course and the top reel was spinning uselessly while empty white light poured from the lens.) Trotting toward him, I wondered how to solicit his attention. I have always been confused as to how one addresses people one doesn't know. Hey, buddy? Hey, Mac? Hey, pal? The "hey" seemed fairly constant so I contented myself with that. "Hey," I called, "just a second. I want to talk to you."

The elevator had just opened and he had backed into it, pulling the cart in after him. It was one of those elevators whose doors seem terribly anxious to close as quickly as possible and, luckily for me, the doors hit the cart and grudgingly opened again just as I caught up to him. "Where are you taking those?" I asked him, holding on to the door and applying all my strength to keep it from closing.

He looked pretty rattled, though I couldn't tell whether it was me or the elevator that was upsetting him. His thin lips had the sheen of eggplant skin and they twitched nervously. "Let me alone," he said.

"Where are you taking those?" I repeated. I noticed that my folder was on the top of the heap and I grabbed it. "Who sees these?" I asked, shaking the folder.

The poor man must have been tottering for quite some time because my faint threat toppled him. He squeezed his hands together and his milky eyes rolled around in his head like a cartoon patsy's just after a sledgehammer blow. "No rough stuff," he asked. "Let's just take it easy."

"I'm just asking a question," I said, slightly alarmed at the thought of violence. "Who sees these, now? Worthington or Simon? I've got a perfect right to know."

He was pressed flat against the elevator wall. "Neither," he said in an exceedingly small voice.

"Then who?" I said, feeling my strength.

"Most of them just get burned unread. I take them to be burned." He was practically weeping from fear.

I was in no shape to press my advantage just then. "What?" I said, stepping back. "What?"

As soon as I stepped back he pulled in the cart the rest of the way and the elevator doors closed with a quick clap, as if dismissing me.

The elevator was operated with a key I did not possess so I could not pursue the old man. I slammed my fists rather hard against the smooth green doors for a few seconds and then, without really thinking, I began to run toward the west wing, where there was an elevator I could operate. I wanted to see Mr. Worthington immediately. My only theory was that he was being victimized by some dreadful middle-management conspiracy and was deprived of the lion's share of the data being produced. What did I care? Was I sucking up to him? Well, these questions did not present themselves to me and if they had I'm certain I would have sidestepped them with precious little thought, for what concerned me then (as now) were certain irritating irregularities in NESTER's functioning, gaps, nonsequiturs, breaks in the film.

I took the elevator down to the computer center and found the next elevator, with Mr. Worthington's initial, which would take me the rest of my descent. Unfortunately, I had no electromagnetic doodad with which to open the doors and no sooner did I ponder that than the doors slid miraculously open and who should emerge but a small, European-looking man whom I could have sworn was Carl Stein. I stared at him and he seemed more than faintly surprised to see me — but maybe he was merely a stranger taken aback by my hot stare. He wore a top coat and a hat and everything happened so quickly. How could it have been Stein?

But I did not ponder. My foremost thought was to catch the elevator doors before they closed. Succeeding in this, I leaned against the wall and scrunched my feet into the fur-carpeted floor. Lights flashed on and off. The elevator reached its destination, discharged me, and I went directly to the speeding yellow car which would carry me the length of the chill tunnel to Mr. W.'s lair. Again, I enjoyed the ride.

Miss Andrews spotted me from her glass cubicle and her features did nothing to suppress the alarm she felt upon seeing me. Not wanting to give her time to react or concoct, I leaped from the Krazy Kar and bounded forward. "I want to see Mr. Worthington," I said, rushing her. Before she could answer, I turned and saw the door leading to his inner office. Abandoning fear, sense, and self-preservation, I threw it open and entered.

Mr. W. sat at his desk, his hands behind his head, and he seemed to be breathing rather heavily. His face was damp and for a moment it seemed as if he'd just been weeping, but, looking more closely and coming a little closer to my senses, I realized he had merely washed his face. "I'm sorry to burst in," I said, quickly establishing both my lowliness and culpability.

He merely nodded.

"But there's something I need to know," I continued. "I just received some upsetting information."

"What have you heard, Paul?"

"Someone told me that the weekly reports were going to be burned."

"And?"

"*And?*" I shook my head. "I thought you should know."

Mr. Worthington sighed and leaned forward onto his desk. He looked as if he were about to say something but then he raised his hand and pressed his fingers against his eyes. He seemed to be mumbling to himself.

"What's that, Mr. Worthington?" I asked.

He looked up at me. "With what agonizing slowness do people change. With what thunderous stupidity and vanity do they live their days."

"I don't know, Mr. Worthington," I said in my best teen-age voice.

"Please, Paul, leave me alone. This is one of my sad days. This is one of my throw-in-the-towel days."

"But what about the reports?"

"I'm aware of what happens in these offices, Paul. Far more aware than you are. The time when you come bursting in here to tell *me* what's going on is a long way off."

"Are you telling me that I work up those reports just to feed some damn fire?"

He rose slowly from his chair and stood behind his desk with his hands at his side. Not quite looking at me, he said, "Of course not, Paul. Why would I permit such a thing?" He folded his hands, raised his eyebrows, and tilted his head to the side. "Now, please. I need silence

138

and solitude and I need it now. And you, I am sure you have much to do. We have given you enough to keep three men busy. We'll talk again. Soon." As if on cue, his phone rang and he picked it up quickly. "Hello?" he said into the receiver.

I stood there for a few moments, working my jaw back and forth and trying to formulate one piercing question that would open an avenue to that old man, that cart filled with reports, that gentleman with the overcoat and the uncanny resemblance to the former Carl Stein. But at the same time there was a mixture of humming and ringing in my ears, my mouth was so dry it felt I had been chewing on a wad of cotton, and there seemed a good possibility I might collapse in a quivering, confused heap at any moment. So, rather than make any more of a display of myself, I turned on my heel. "Wait a minute, now. Just slow down," Mr. Worthington said. I turned around with a start, but he was talking to whoever it was on the other end of the line.

9

I AWOKE TODAY and how pure and clear my life seemed. How shabby and hesitant I had been up until now. It is no longer a matter for conjecture: I am not much longer for this life. My time with NESTER is drawing to a close. I washed my face and looked in the mirror. Behind that mirror may be cameras, my toothbrush may be a microphone, every inch of my biologic territory may be at this very moment totally overrun by information-seeking hordes, carrying away the bounty of my secret self. I smiled at myself in the mirror above the sink, letting the toothpaste fall carelessly from my mouth. With a haircut, a shave, and a conservative tie I would be more than ready to testify before that quaking congressional committee.

In the meantime, I have developed talents of my own. Yes. I will not be easy prey. I have learned to create a counterpunctual screen for my most compromising thoughts. Even blatant brain thievery would fail to

140

discern what I am thinking about. For instance, I may be thinking about what a miserable creep Tom Simon is — not that I would give him any thought, but let's just toss that out for an example. Well, simultaneously with the formation of that attitude I am reciting the results of classical experiments in neurophysiology or simply counting to 99 by threes. In the forefront of my consciousness is always some diverting bit of irrelevance, while the thoughts that are most vital to me are like shadows on the water, sensed more than seen. My brain has become a cryptogram, opaque and impossible for the malicious probings of your average brain thief. As I write these very words I am deeply engrossed in a slew of innocuous childhood memories, having to do with bicycles and biscuits and frosty Thanksgiving afternoons. Everything I want to say is stored in my finger tips, is beeping in the marrow of my bones, and all my brain needs to do is direct the elementary pull and tug of muscle necessary to move my pen.

I must write very slowly. I shudder to think this may be all illegible. That I will be found, monstrous and dead, in the Charles River and all the inquest will turn up is this notebook filled with indecipherable scrawlings. There is very little light. I am taking extreme caution. We were saying our prayers and Grandfather said his eyes were turning cold, his eyes were freezing right in their sockets. I am under my blankets, lying on my stomach. There is a crack of light to my left where I have raised the blanket about a quarter of an inch. The only other light is the luminous face of my wrist watch which I move down the page as I write this.

The final problem is that of audio detection. No matter how light my touch, there is a certain sound that a pen makes when it glides, no matter how gracefully, over paper and I must conceal this sound. So I am under my blankets, I am writing by the luminous face of my wrist watch — with not enough light actually to read my words but sufficient glow to make certain that I am writing on the lines of my ruled paper — and to cover the tiny hiss of pen on paper I am humming to myself. Rock-a-byes, hit tunes, nursery rhymes, anything with a simple, lilting melody. Somewhere unseen eyes, unseen ears are taking all this in. They see me in my dark room, huddled beneath my blankets. I am projected on the screen to their left. They are wearing earphones and they hear I am humming, la-la-la-ing. They probably take me for crazy. All of my cousins had bicycles before I did but did *their* eyes open when I finally unveiled my crimson beauty, and how the spokes sparkled in the sun as I wheeled it in a slow circle for their envious amazement.

◆ ◆ ◆

Sitting at my desk, leafing through some new print-outs on the sexing experiments, fantasizing about an escape and a new life, and wondering if I was being watched, I lifted my head and opened my eyes wider. I had recently spilled a half cup of coffee onto the floor and at my feet was a soggy mass of paper napkins. Did I, I wondered, seem a trustworthy employee to the casual company spy? Was I photogenic? I filled my mind with extraneous information, hastily assembled trains of thought — thoughts of baseball box scores and Colonial history, memories of the mambo and English formal gardens, anything to present a neutral neuronal appearance if my brain waves were being zeroed in on.

It was the first of June and, I was soon to discover, my day to go into town. I had completely lost track of the days and had no idea it was my day to go to Boston. But my door suddenly flew open (not only was my heart in my mouth but I'd say my liver and pancreas were up there, too) and there they were, three of my coworkers and a Force Recruiter (recently retired from active duty) who was to act as our chauffeur, which meant in actuality he was to make certain all of us refrained from accosting strangers with pleading, wild tales and came back. "Come on, come on, hurry up, please," said Freddy McCarthy, beside himself with excitement. They were peering at me anxiously. I shuffled my papers and blinked back at them, cursing myself for not having prepared for the outing. Perhaps it was the day for my escape — I could leap out of the car at a red light and tear ass through Back Bay, ducking into luncheonettes, barreling through alleyways, waving my arms and screaming. But even such a chaotic escape takes a certain amount of cunning and forethought and this excursion caught me unawares. It would be a month before a similar opportunity presented itself to me . . .

I looked up and smiled, a faintly sick expression on my face. Our keeper, a burly old French-Canadian named Toulouse, stroked the ends of his white mustache and moved his muscles in a rippling warning beneath his short-sleeved, yellow Ban-lon turtleneck shirt.

In the car, a white Buick, there was an inordinate

143

amount of horsing around, so excited were my coworkers about their little excursion. Normally, I share in this general gaiety but today I sat pressed far back in the seat, not talking, not smiling, barely blinking, my mind trembling with plans and revelations. Freddy McCarthy and Buddy Herzberg played Botticelli with a new psychologist, a birdish, prematurely bald boy with a rasping voice whose name was Ferris Ohnsorg. To add to the fun of the game, the new boy answered all their questions in a mock Mexican accent. Is it a movie star, they would ask, and he would answer, "No, seenyour, eat eaze not Seed Chyrisse," and the three of them would grin silently.

And so we cruised, the Force Recruiter firmly at the wheel, past small suburban plots.

A horse, a bar and grill, a father and two daughters playing basketball in their driveway, which held a white Buick exactly like the one that took us so quickly past them, a billboard advertising a downtown Boston hotel, a gas station — all of those worldly sights and hundreds more glided gently by me, softened and prismatically brilliant through a nostalgic mist. I wiped my eyes, dabbed at my tear ducts with the pads of my trembling fingers, and lowered my head. Toulouse readjusted the rearview mirror.

We entered Boston, made our way down Storrow Drive, and haggled with each other over how the day would be spent. We all had money to burn. Toulouse had given each of us a lime green envelope filled with cash. There were many things I wanted to buy: expensive pens, a terrific watch, jackets, paints, art books, a gun. We had previously agreed that we would all see a new

144

Dirk Bogarde movie, but that would take us only to 1:49. We had between then and six o'clock to do whatever else we wanted.

The arguments were nagging and hostile, the suggestions shrill. You wouldn't have believed the demands, the threats, the wheedling. Toulouse puffed on a Gauloise in contemptuous silence. One of us wanted to go see where a strange hippie cult lived on Mission Hill, one wanted to shop for antique bottles, someone else wanted to ride the swan boats in the Public Garden; then one wanted to wander around Harvard, one wanted to sample organic restaurants — one wanted this, one wanted that. All brain thieves, I suppose, are a little desperate and compulsive. We were irreconcilable. Tempers flared. Ferris was practically in tears. Toulouse was just driving around the block, listening to us make fools of ourselves. We were confirming every dirty little story a Force Recruiter had ever heard about a psychologist.

On his third time around the block that contained the movie theater we had agreed on going to, I noticed an elegant-looking stationery store and remembered how I yearned for expensive pens. I screamed for him to stop, which much to my surprise he did. At my urgent bidding, we all piled out of the car and went into the store — it seems pointless, but where one goes all must follow, as if we were a road gang.

It was a small store, meticulously arranged with a thousand crannies and shelves, dimly lit, and presided over by a heavyset woman in her early seventies, who wore a long-sleeved rose-colored dress and wheezed uncomfortably. She must have been a little startled to see us charge into

145

her shop (which she probably ran for the sake of privacy), and her milky eyes surveyed us with bulbous anxiety as I bought pen after costly pen and my coworkers stood along the wall sighing impatiently.

◆ ◆ ◆

I returned from Boston and stumbled into my room. My arms were loaded with the purchases of a free-spending afternoon and I dropped everything in a heap on the faintly dusty floor and threw myself onto my narrow, unmade bed. My interior decorations, normally a matter of utter indifference to me, struck me as sad and repellent as I surveyed the circumscribed quarters I was forced to call home. The lights, for example, were poorly, almost aggressively placed, casting metallic shafts in certain areas and leaving other patches in a kind of dank, gray half light. Since my windows do not open, my room had not known fresh air since its completion and the air that was pumped in by the ventilation system gave the place the feel of the Holland Tunnel, only cooler.

I had spent $500 on new clothes. I had successfully bullied my colleagues into going to some of Boston's better stores and I had bought an English suit, a pair of gray, delicate shoes, and a blue hat with a yellow band, quite similar to the one depicted in my Van Gogh print, worn by that neutral boy with the heartbreaking mustache. Perhaps, I thought, looking at the boxes and bags I had dumped onto the floor and resolving with an inward groan to hang up my things, perhaps I should grow a mustache. Anything.

I thought of my suit, my shoes, my hat, my gloves, my

socks, my handkerchiefs, my tube of West German aftershave cream, and then there was an exceedingly effacing knock at my door. I was too tired and too demoralized to muster my usual torrents of fear and I merely groaned, "Come in."

There entered a short, stout man wearing a multicolored shirt, which made him look something akin to an Easter egg. His face, however, was gray and forlorn. Suffering, one might say. He was at least fifty years old and the turn of his mouth was positively ulcerous. His skin was deeply creased and his large pale eyes were intersected by thunderbolts of red. "Hello," he said in a grating voice.

"Why . . . hello," I said, sitting up.

"I've just been put on your visiting schedule," he rasped. "My name is Dr. Popkoff." He closed the door behind him and walked stiffly toward me with his hand extended.

I stood up and shook his hand, a small cold thing with steely fingers. "Pleased to meet you," I said, staring at him. I had never before been visited and exploding through the fatigue that had moments ago blanketed my senses was a small sense of cunning and a large dose of dread. Why was this man in my room? I sat at the edge of my bed. Popkoff plopped on the couch.

"I've seen you in the cafeteria," he parried.

"I eat there," said I.

"Yes," he agreed, nodding solemnly. Two or three minutes of silence ensued.

"Is there anything special?" I asked finally. He was sitting with his legs crossed, his hands folded in his lap, his chin dropped onto his chest, and I felt he might soon drift off.

"Hmmm?" he said, jerking up his head and forcing a smile. His teeth were enormous and a couple of them flashed in the light.

"I wondered why you decided to stop by," I said, rephrasing my question and frowning at him.

"Mr. Worthington suggested I stop by and have a chat with you," Popkoff replied with surprising candor.

"Oh?" I managed to say, an eagle taking flight in my digestive tract.

He nodded and sighed, shrugged, and lifted his hands. His hands fell back onto his lap and he said, "I'm a pharmacologist. I'm adviser on the Pandium project."

"What are you talking about?" I said, feeling suddenly reckless and strong.

"Pandium? Oh, that's a new drug I've — we've developed. Part barbiturate, part stimulant, part hypnotic, part transistor. We sell them to the Now Generation."

"The 'Now Generation'?" I repeated, with a mocking voice and a grimace.

"You know," Popkoff pled.

"I'm sure I haven't the slightest idea what you're talking about." I felt good now. I was smart, tough, and composed.

"The kids. The dopers. We sell it to them and then they're ours. No surgery necessary. No force recruiting. They're just a swallow away."

"Impressive," I said.

"Oh . . . yes," he said, "it's really something." His hand went to his forehead and he tugged at the skin

148

there. His large, moist lower lip quivered perceptibly. A long, whistling, piercing sigh escaped from him.

"What's the matter?" I asked, leaning forward.

"Matter? Oh, tired I guess. Very . . . tired. Sometimes I think — " and here he clenched his teeth — "they do everything in their power to drive us mad."

My palms moistened in response to his treasonous remark. However, I was far from convinced by it. I remembered that when *I* was running errands for Mr. W. making treasonous remarks was one of *my* techniques. "What do you mean?" I asked in a neutral voice.

"I'm crazy for saying this," he began, "but the way this place is run strikes me as cruel and unnecessary punishment."

"Punishment?"

"Certainly. The regulations, the isolation, the tempo. And the experiments themselves. I'm so sad."

"You are?"

He nodded. "I've been here six years. I'm bored to the brink of madness. Whatever made me think I'd be interested in these experiments? I feel really only revulsion over them. I'm making a huge salary, but what good does all the gold in the kingdom do me when I can't swim in the pool here because my eyes flare up from the chlorine?"

"I'm quite happy here," I countered cagily.

"I know, I know. That's why Mr. Worthington suggested I come to see you. I've been — been spouting off about this for quite some time now and I've even spoken to my superiors about it. He told me you were particularly happy here — though not without your difficulties

— and that it would be helpful for me to speak with you."

He heaved another deep sigh, slapped his hands onto his knees, and stood up. "They told me in the beginning," he said, pacing about, "that there'd be a period of adjustment and I was to be patient. But now I'm quite accustomed to everything and it's no better for me, no easier. Worse, actually. I don't enjoy the experiments. Perhaps if they gave me something new to do, something bigger. I guess all of us had our plans and dreams about what we'd like to be doing when we reached a place like NESTER. We are all of us ambitious people. But they don't tell you everything. It's really a goddamned bureaucracy. Memos, appointments, protocol, secrecy — I wanted to live in a community of scholars and technicians, and instead I end up in some ten-foot-square room with faulty ventilation. I wanted to sit beneath redwood trees in a pair of madras shorts and have leisurely, important conversations with my intellectual peers, but instead I find myself isolated, under constant suspicion, stymied, and the only recreations I get — well, I told you about the pool. Look at my eyes! I spend half my time in the infirmary getting treatments for them. God!" His fists went to the sides of his head and remained there for a few long moments, as if he were posing for a picture. "It's not worth it," he said, his voice shattering. "It's not worth all of their money, it's not worth their seventy-five thousand dollars a year. It's not worth their . . ."

But I lost track of what followed, so astonished was I to hear that the pissed-off Popkoff was pulling in a full thirty-five thousand dollars more a year than I was. Not that such things mattered so awfully much — I was leaving NESTER, about to blow it wide open, and even if I wasn't there was little opportunity to spend and enjoy one's money while slaving away here — but it was sobering to realize just how much a toad they had played me for.

"It's not worth their —" he was saying.

"Well, just what in the hell are you going to do about it?" I interrupted, pounding my fist into my open hand and jutting out my lower lip.

"What *can* I do? As I've been told, I'm not the first person here to become unhappy about the situation I find myself in. But what am I supposed to do about it? I'm seeing a psychiatrist three times a week — fifty bucks a throw. I'm trying to teach myself yoga and meditation. I do a little watercoloring but I don't have any talent and my pictures are morbid." Suddenly he stopped his shrugging and pacing, looked at me with cold, frightened eyes, and said, "I think about escape."

"Oh?" If indeed I had at that point been hooked up to a NESTER-ine recording device I think my convulsive reaction to the word "escape" might have short-circuited several sophisticated barometers.

"Yes, yes, yes, I do," he said with a frightening wildness coursing over his features. "I see myself in dreams riding in a car, beneath a low sky filled with clouds and World War One-type airplanes and I am listening to the radio and my arm is around a young woman and we are talking about where to stop for our picnic. This is a dream I have often. The sky grows lighter as I continue on. But no one leaves here, of that I'm quite certain. The doors are locked. There are guards before each one. The lawn is undoubtedly electrified. There are probably search-lights and machine guns surrounding this place." He lifted his eyes and I noticed a wormish pink scar along the side of his throat. He rubbed his hands together and sat down. He swallowed, tried to get a grip on himself. "Well," he said, "what do you think?"

"What do I think?"

"Yes. What's your impression? What's your advice?"

"I think you should put all foolish thoughts out of your mind," I said very slowly. It was perhaps a cruel thing to say but I could take no chances. My freedom was worth more than his peace of mind. There was, first of all, no reason to believe in Popkoff's legitimacy — I myself had gone on these investigative missions for Mr. W. — and even if Popkoff's agony were genuine he would benefit, in the long run, more from my eventual escape and worldwide prominence than he would from a few kind words. "There is no chance of your leaving here," I continued. "No one has ever left NESTER, unless the people in charge have chosen so."

"I know, I know," he said forlornly, shaking his head. "But how I yearn to be on my own. How I long to see old friends — friends with whom I had really very little in common but whose memories now haunt me and fill me with unbearable sadness. I would like to see my wife — her name is Jane and I never loved her, at least I thought I never loved her. But now, here, after all this time, I see her face, even smell her. I wonder where she is. She has probably remarried. An attractive woman, beset with annoying yet forgivable habits. We were childless. She has now probably a dozen children. She is English."

152

"She couldn't possibly have a dozen children," I said. "You haven't been away that long."

"Yes, of course. How silly of me," he said, taking no particular comfort in the fact.

"And you've no reason to believe she's remarried at all," I said. "She may choose to spend the rest of her life in solitude."

"Is that what your wife chose?"

"What makes you think I was married?"

"Mr. Worthington told me. Her name is . . . Lydia? Do you think she now lives in solitude?"

I experienced an unpleasant, queer feeling, like a small elevator rising up from the base of my neck through my skull. "I don't know," I said a trifle breathlessly. "I don't think about it. About her. I'm a better brain thief than I was a husband."

"Brain thief?" He paused for a moment. "Oh, yes. I see. Well, yes, I suppose that's the position most of us find ourselves in. Fantasies about returning to one's old life or even beginning a new one *are* rather stifled by the realization that one has never done anything but one's work with any degree of competency, that one's personal life has been a washout, that friendships, marriages, and even casual relationships lie behind one in shambles. That one has taken no joy in either God or Nature or even, for that matter, organized sports. That one's dreams had always been riddled with yearnings for unwholesome power, unreasonable influence."

"Well," I said, "you seem to have it pretty much figured out. With such a sensible analysis of your situation here I don't see how you allow yourself these dreams of escap-

153

ing, of finding yourself still another life. Why don't you just accept what you have?"

"I knew you'd say that," he said, getting up.

"What else *can* I say?" I said flatly, absurdly hoping that if he were on my side he would sense I was on his.

Both of our faces drained of expression, as if we both simultaneously remembered the tucked-away cameras that were recording our engineered encounter. The next cameras, I vowed, that I would stand before would be television cameras at some none too distant press conference where I spilled the brain-picking beans to a slack-jawed room of reporters.

"May I come to see you again?" Popkoff asked, moving toward the door.

"Whenever you like."

He opened the door. "Thank you. And you may, quite naturally, drop into my room whenever you choose. I feel there's more to say about this matter. I'm on the ground floor — I've no view at all. Room one-twelve. How ironic that they put me there. Perhaps they knew when I came here that I'd have dreams of flight as soon as my dreams of pharmacological power had been fulfilled. I mean, my room is right next to a main exit. No one guards it except an old man named Mr. Acoraci. He's all that stands between me and the great outdoors." Popkoff shook his head. "But I'll never leave. So what's the use?" He closed the door behind him without a good-bye.

My head was pounding from the strain of his visit. The pressure of listening to him, answering him, and camou-flaging my real thoughts had strung electric wires of pain about my skull and I was weak from it. I paced the room.

154

I heard voices, noises, sounds, scrapes. The ticking of a clock sounded like water dripping on a microphone. I put my hands over my ears and it was louder still.

I knew in the marrow of my bones that I was on my way out. Suddenly, the moves and the countermoves meant very little to me. I was on my way. Soon. Now. Tomorrow. I briefly reflected on the world I was going to see, the natural wonders, the human misery. And suddenly my room took on a surreal clarity — my life was supernatural. I threw open the door and looked down the empty corridors. From behind closed doors I heard muffled conversations. I closed the door after me and strode through the halls, swinging my arms and breathing deeply. I wanted to take it all in. The porcelain drinking fountains, the faintly antiseptic odor. I arrived at the stairway and decided to trot up to my office.

I opened up the frosted glass door, the neon lights shook the room back and forth as they struggled to turn on, and I sat on the couch and looked around. My office, too, was wild with previously unperceived life. Objects seemed to tremble, others appeared to glow. Then I noticed there were scuff marks on the woodwork going all around the room, as if someone had been kicking at it. I had never done any kicking in my office. It must have been a previous tenant. It was funny I had never noticed them before. I had also never noticed that the color of the woodwork was lemon yellow, which exactly matched the color of the ceiling. That was pretty obvious but I had never noticed it, or it never registered. The couch I sat on was covered in some kind of plastic and the plastic was cracked, from heat or wear, and the seat

155

was traversed by thousands of delicate lines. I stood up and, as if by inspiration, I figured out why my desk wobbled. There was a screw right in the center that attached the desk top to its mount and that screw had worked itself loose — or was it sabotage? I dropped to my knees and tightened the screw with my hands, covering my finger tips with my handkerchief.

The whole cubicle had come alive for me, as if my senses had thawed. After all these months. Years! I wasn't used to it, wasn't equipped. I walked over to my window. It was twenty minutes before nine o'clock and I watched the summer night close over the last bit of sun. The window threw my reflection at me, as if my image had been summoned by the night. As it grew darker my reflection grew sharper. I looked at my sad, practically dead eyes with eerie objectivity. I had, I said aloud, bitten off more than I cared to chew. I slowly rubbed the back of my head. My eyebrows, I noticed, were growing together a little. That would have to be taken care of. "My name is Paul Lloyd Galambos," I whispered, momentarily enshrouding my reflection with my hot breath. Quickly, the light film of steam evaporated and I saw a lone young tree at the far end of the NESTER compound bend in the wind like a servant girl. No, much more graceful than that — a ballerina. I was no longer bothering to conceal my thoughts. My synapses were humming with anticipation, with vague plans for flight. By the time my thoughts had been processed and deciphered I would be gone. I must get out of here. That's what I thought. Unadorned, unmistakable, a direct statement. It filled my head like a gaudy red balloon.

10

LOOKING BACK ON IT NOW (months have passed and I have learned to write left-handed) I dwell on the rather meaningless fact that I never bothered to open my packages of clothes, never tried on that English suit or that blue and yellow wide-brimmed hat. Now in tatters, living alone in the heart of this country — and the heart, my friends, is barely beating, the heart in fact has stopped — I think back to those dandy duds and in my feverish and secretive mind they take on an onerous, symbolic load they were never meant to carry and under which they collapse in an exhausted, depleted heap.

I will abandon those clothes in that room and with them I will similarly ditch any impulse that tempts me even momentarily from the barest thread of my narrative. What happened that night and the long, humid day that followed it will be enough to explain for one man, and a broken, profoundly confused man at that.

I have been leafing through this journal preparing for

this, my final entry. Some of it is frankly illegible and perhaps may never be deciphered. Some of it pulls me back to those days on the outskirts of Boston, puts me in that speeding subterranean car, in that office, beneath that desk. But what most magically conjures that final evening are the two long, wide strips of pale blue on the journal's navy blue cover, the remnants of the tape with which I secured the notebook to my back right before I bolted. Looking at those long skid marks, I can see myself shirtless in the harsh light of my sleeping quarters, my chest heaving, a glacial pool of perspiration forming in the small of my back, my eyes as large as walnuts. I was taping the journal to my back, reeling with the vague, absurd hope that if I were to be gunned down or drowned the journal might be discovered and would tell the story in my place. (Brief fantasies of a hero's burial: pan shots of weeping crowds, my wife, desolate and red-eyed, leaning on two secret service agents.) I put down my pen and run my fingers over those bald strips.

It will take me years, it seems, to learn to write properly with my left hand. But I don't mind. It's something to do.

All right. Enough.

After I taped my journal to my back I put on my shirt. I was wearing a dark blue shirt and black pants — quite by coincidence, but they were perfect for slithering through the nighttime lawn on my way to some superhighway. I thought about Popkoff's projections of NESTER security: the machine gun turret with the curls of ammunition on the perforated metal floor, the searchlight roaming ominously through the night, illuminating here

158

a phalanx of moths and there a retreating heel. I had to move fast. There was no doubt in my mind that I had been for quite some time under observation — my hope was, in fact, that my observers had contented themselves with tape recorders and cameras and had not gone IN-SIDE for their ill-gotten information — and my only chance was that there was no one directly responsible for the ongoing cameras and such but that they were emptied of their revelations every morning or so by a low-level functionary who brought them to someone else for cursory examination. I thought for a moment about that shuffling lackey, rising at dawn and going from camera to camera for each incriminating cassette and dropping them into an aluminum basket with the nonchalance of a peasant gathering unbreakable eggs. I waved good-bye to a point in the wall where I felt the camera may have been placed.

I decided to take nothing with me. I didn't want to be slowed down and I had, I think, the foolish, degrading idea that if I were apprehended in the halls or on the grounds I could get away with saying I was merely taking a stroll. I had no money. Since there was nothing within the compound to spend money on we were given our cash only on outing days and after the outing it was recollected from us. It made it more difficult to take little outings on one's own.

There followed fifteen minutes of hopeless fright.

Finally, I had composed myself sufficiently to open up my door and peek down the corridor. Droning in the nether lands of thought were Popkoff's observations which, if taken at face value, added up virtually to instructions to me. He had said he was in Room 112. On the ground floor. Next to a main exit. Only one guard. An old man. Mr. Acoraci! My faith in these instructions was far from secure: it existed like the yolk of a frying egg whose perimeter quivers incessantly, always just about to splash open and run helplessly into the seething, crackling white that surrounds it. But it was the only hope, the only plan I had. I closed the door behind me and stepped into the hall.

Running on tiptoe past the rows of closed doors — every so often a shaft of yellow light would spill from beneath one of them and I would hop over it — I made my way to the stairwell. Holding on to the smooth, chilly banister, I ran down the stairs. I had decided speed was my friend. There was no percentage in creeping about, of lurking in corners, of hiding behind fire extinguishers. Just go, go quickly. I reached the bottom of the stairs and stood before a double lime green door: ground floor. I pressed against one of the doors. It did not budge. I clenched my hands and looked upward — five flights of flat gray stairs grew toward the roof in right angles. I saw myself racing up them, finding some trap door to the roof, and leaping into the — I leaned against the other half of the swinging door and it opened easily.

Above me, a flourescent square of light quivered and the corridor, encompassed in its stuttering illumination, jerked and swayed. Resisting a tidal wave of nausea, I made my way down the freshly waxed hall, my leather soles slipping dangerously here and there. Soon I came upon Room 112. I filled with fury. I thought of Popkoff's information and fatefully accepted the possibility that as I passed his door it would fly open and from it would pour a trio of heavies who would pummel me floorward. Well, fuck them, I thought with anger and stupidity. There was every reason to believe that each piece of Popkoffian perfidy had been constructed as a clumsy yet effective trap into which yours truly was inexorably stumbling, but personal safety seemed, at that stage, a heavily shrouded concept, essentially incomprehensible to my excited senses. I even momentarily considered opening Room 112 myself, saying good-bye to morose Dr. P., or inviting him to come along with me, or telling him to keep heart and trust me eventually to get him out of the mess he was in, or spitting on his floor. But as I glanced at the frosted glass window on his door I noticed to my left a small red and black sign: EXIT. And beneath that sign was a small old man in a militarily cut lime green uniform, replete with black-billed cap and brass buttons. He sat at a table which was bare save an enormous black telephone. He was staring at me with torrid little eyes.

I approached him. "Hi," I said, grinning.

He placed his powder white hands on the beige table.

"You're Mr. Acoraci, aren't you?" I asked, swaying back and forth and trying to think of something else to say.

"Lemme see your assignmenting papers," he said in a small meanish voice.

I wasn't certain what he meant. "I don't have them with me. But I'm on an important assignment. Project number four-fifty-six-w-twenty-one, if you know what I mean."

"Sorry," he said, "I don't let no one out without seeing the papers and then I call." He looked at me suspiciously. "Don't you know that?"

My leg muscles tightened. I had to get out. A quick,

clumsy plan developed. I leaned toward the old man and with one finger tipped his hat off his head. It bounced onto the floor, quivered for a moment, and then was still. Acoraci looked at me with the indignant anger of the very old. As he leaned over to pick up his hat I took the telephone receiver off the hook and smacked him with it on the top of his head. Three times, maybe four. The receiver, now partially red, dangled from the table as I raced toward the door.

I pressed down on the silver bar and it opened to the night, the stars, and all my dreams of freedom.

I scarcely knew what was happening anymore. Instinctively, I ran toward the sounds of the highway. The lawn was damp and squeaked beneath my frantic footfalls. I tripped over a garden hose and fell face forward onto the moist green grass. I stayed there for a moment, enamored by the cool, sweet aroma. Scrambling up, I chanced a quick glance behind me. No guards came forth with fixed bayonets, no finger of light leafed curiously through the pages of night. My breath was coming in spurts. I found myself in a half-empty parking lot. A band of pain wrapped itself around my abdomen. It had been months since I'd run. Decades. I was giggling. I couldn't believe how easy it had been. I couldn't believe it had actually happened.

A small, grassy knoll presented itself and I ran over to it. There before me, perhaps fifteen yards below my not very imposing perch, lay the highway, a bright gray strip of concrete with luminous markers on either side that were ignited by the headlights of every passing car. I had no idea which way it was to town. I closed my eyes and tried to remember that morning's outing. The big white Buick . . . but replacing the chic, toothy car in my mind's wide eye was a vision of that dangling red telephone and Mr. Acoraci slumping slack-jawed to the floor.

I skidded down the knoll and tried to flag down a car, for a minute abandoning concern over my destination. Cars whizzed by, buffeting me with the air they displaced. I heard the sound of a siren and, after buckling momentarily from the force of a cardiovascular contraction, I dived into a mane of free-growing weeds at the side of the road. The whooping grew louder and soon I saw spots of red light dancing over the surface of the road and, as a few courteous motorists pulled to the side, an ambulance flashed past. My shirt was wet from the moisture of the earth and my socks were, too.

I scrambled up. I was shivering, a little. Two diesel trucks roared by, filling my ears with their smoky confusion and shaking the ground beneath me. I began to run. Before I tried to get a ride, I wanted to get further from the compound. As I trotted along the pebbly roadside I made ineffectual arm gestures at passing cars, which the drivers either ignored or were repelled by. When I had run about 500 yards I stopped and tried seriously to flag down a whizzing motorist. I waved my arms over my head and leaned into the road as if I were at any moment about to baptize myself in that stream of traffic. No one stopped. I whistled and shouted; my energetic waving had pulled my shirttails from my trousers. No one stopped. Some drivers, though not many, would stare curiously at me. One man shouted something from the safety of his speeding vehicle.

I decided I looked too strange to be picked up. Too frantic, too close to the edge. Then I had a bit of rare good luck. Before me, about fifty yards away, was an abandoned car. It was quite badly damaged and had been vandalized, but I figured if I stood near it — though not *too* near — I might be mistaken for a motorist in distress and that role and situation would be familiar enough to convince some benevolent soul to interrupt his or her journey momentarily and take me along.

As I stood there with my thumb extended, I wished I were part of something larger, something organized, some well-ordered conspiracy. I hadn't stopped dreaming. I wished there had been, say, a mouse gray Rolls ready to scoop me up and away to safety. A steady driver with a cloth cap, and someone from the press, and a blond woman with skinny legs. They all should have been there, waiting. That would have been perfect. As it was, it was chaos. Uncomfortable and unlikely. "Step on it," the emaciated Danish lady would have said . . . Cars roared by me. It wasn't, I realized, terribly far to Boston, but I didn't have the strength to walk. I barely felt the strength to stand. I was terrified of being apprehended, afraid of that car, or that one, or the next one stopping and unloosing a seething claque of armed heavies who would shower me with rabbit punches and drag me back to NESTER. I yearned for the city, where I'd have a better chance to hide, to escape, and to implement my plan of alerting and informing the world of my crimes through the medium of the international press. Cars of all makes and models flashed past. I was passed by snazzy Peugeots and dumpy Volkswagens, a type of car, we have

164

discovered, that holds particular appeal for men domi-
nated by women. Rebels, Chargers, Mavericks, Comets,
Galaxies, Mustangs, Stingrays, Barracudas, and Grem-
lins all passed Paul Galambos by. I was passed by trucks
carrying horses, trucks carrying turnips, trucks carrying
oil, bottled water, lumber, and baby food. I was passed
by jeeps. My hands were briefly illuminated by a pair of
headlights and I noticed my fingers had wispy red smears
on them. I cleaned them by spitting on them and wiping
them on the starlit grass.

♦　♦　♦

I've had to take a rest. I thought I could spew this
whole thing out in one shimmering aqua stream, but my
left hand has developed none of the endurance necessary
to write more than an hour or so at a time and I am too
broke (not to say broken) to afford even a tiny typewriter.
I've had it with machines, anyhow.
But I've been exercising it, my hand that is, faithfully.
As I walk the boring streets of this faintly hostile town I
am squeezing a salmon-colored rubber ball, past the Variety Store, past the Jewel Supermarket, out toward the outskirts of town where I am momentarily joined by a curious
black dog with a sooty bandage on its left front paw. Sun-
set. The cornfields turning purple.
As I was saying, a car finally did stop for me on that
starry, frightened night. It stopped about fifty feet beyond me (it was a light blue compact and it stopped with
a series of short hops toward the side of the road) and I
ran to it with entrancing visions of myself sitting in a Senate office behind a crescent of microphones. I had played

out this self-serving fantasy many times and it was reaching one of its predictable, ego-maniacal climaxes (the stampede of roaring reporters beating their way toward the telephones in the back of the chamber) as I put my hand on the car's door and opened it up. "My car's broken," I said, leaning into the little car and facing the young, bespectacled driver, who tugged thoughtfully on the end of his dark mustache.

"Where you going?" he asked.

"Boston," I said uncertainly.

"O.K. Hop in."

I hopped; oh, did I hop. I practically severed a foot, so anxious was I to get in and get going, so relieved was I that the kindly car was pointed Boston-ward.

I was thinking of adding a bit of suspense to this, of leading you to believe that I somehow made it into town, called the night desk of the Boston *Globe*, arranged for a press conference the very next day, and then spent the night preparing my statement in the Parker House hotel, drafting my statement and making long-distance phone calls. But the terrible truth of the matter is that I didn't get very far. No sooner had the young man pulled back onto the highway — I slouched deep into my seat, getting ready to pass the NESTER complex — than we were struck from the side by a battered maroon station wagon. "Oh, my God," the driver cried, as we spun helplessly toward the gravel and the weeds, "this is my sister's car."

Since I was hunched down in the car's terrycloth-covered seat, the impact shook me only slightly. My would-be rescuer was firmly belted into his seat and he merely doddered as his sister's car swerved this way and that and then finally was creased and crunched by a metal road-side marker. A thin line of inky smoke rose from the hood. Faces from rapidly passing cars stared at us. The aggressive station wagon pulled in behind.

It did not take any special occult abilities to realize that the monstrous maroon car did not simply hold a reckless driver or a drunken construction worker or a careless divorcée, but encapsulated instead a sinister stunt driver in NESTER's employ who had just, with awesome ease, stymied my escape, wrecked my chance for revelation, and, for all I knew, insured my execution. I opened up the door, rolled out of the car, and began to run. "Wait!" screamed the boy. I turned to make an apologetic gesture and saw the maroon station wagon open forth and from it emerge a hulking heavy in a gray suit who began ambling in my direction. He, too, shouted, "Wait!"

I had no choice but to race back toward the NESTER complex. I knew I was sunk but I was determined to make them work for it. I was getting my second wind. My feet pounded onto the undergrowth with vigor and authority. A gust of damp night wind filled my shirt and my hair was blowing wild. BRAIN THIEF RUNS TO WEST COAST IN SEVEN HOURS!

From the darkness, a hand grabbed out at me just as the muted white glow of the compound came into view. I attempted to leap back, but the hand had grabbed me with strength and accuracy and if I were to have escaped it would have meant, literally, leaping out of my shirt. As I squirmed, my captor came into view (a square, stupid face whose blandness was marred only by a sick smile) and he was joined, a second later, by his short, bony assis-

167

tant, who carried, in compensation, an imposing black pistol. "You come with us," said the little one, whose face was as long and narrow as a carton of cigarettes.

The hulking heavy grabbed me under my arm and his (I feared) trigger-happy helper shoved the gun's eager muzzle into the small of my back. Both of them led me over that small grassy knoll, through the parking lot, and toward the very door through which I had so hopefully burst. I knew my number was up. "Are you going to get it," promised the larger of my captors.

"I care," I bravely countered, sneering at him.

The little one jabbed the gun into my spine.

"Stop that," I demanded. I attempted to turn around but his powerful partner held me firmly. He opened the side door to the compound and pushed me in.

Mr. Acoraci was there with seven or eight other people. The old man's lime green uniform was bloody — a streak of red beginning at the collar and ending in a full red moon at the breast — and he dabbed uncertainly at the cut on his head with a rolled up handkerchief. Curiously, the blow to his head had revitalized his Italian accent. "That'sa heem," he said, sounding like Chico Marx.

In less than a second the batch of brutes was upon me. With a sudden surge of courage, speed, and dexterity that I cannot to this day understand, I slipped from the hands of my captors (risking a fiery pellet in my back), sensed a pocket of light in the flying wing of Force Recruiters that closed in upon me, and ran — flew! — down the quiet, brightly lit corridor. "Don't shoot," I heard a voice behind me say, "we got orders not to hurt him." "Oh lemme, lemme," another voice pleaded. I pushed open the door

168

to the stairwell and took the smooth gray steps three at a time.

I reached the fourth floor, where my living quarters had been. I flew blindly, panting, crazy, and scared. I looked for an escape, a hiding place, an ally. Yes! I had an idea. Allies. I would alert my colleagues, organize a general protest, a revolution. I ran down this more familiar corridor, trying to find it within me to howl bloody murder. Arise! Arise! Together we can free ourselves. But all I could manage was a guttural plea for help. I began throwing open doors. Most of the rooms were dark, filled with the sounds of sleeping. In a few, I saw amazed men and a few women looking up from their desks and staring at me with considerable distaste. In one room, the occupant was viewing slides of human eyes in extreme close-up. "You goddamned fool," I said to him, and slammed the door.

I looked up and down the hall and saw no one coming after me. I shoved my hands in my pockets and leaned against the wall; my heart beat out a rapid telegraphy of terror and exhaustion. I shook my head and made my way to my room. Perhaps, I thought, they won't kill me or turn me into the house guinea pig, fouling up my frontal lobes and turning my medulla into community property, and perhaps I will sometime in the not too distant future have another crack at freedom. Maybe, I thought, succumbing to the most unrealistic kind of optimism, I can make a break for it during my next outing to Boston.

I came to room number 162 — my room — and I opened the door. The lights were dim. There was a faint odor of — incense. I looked around the room, closed the door

169

behind me, looked around again, and then saw Mr. Worthington sitting on the edge of my bed, his hands folded primly in his lap. "Mr. Worthington!" I gasped.

He rose quickly and stretched his arms out to me. He glided across the small, jumbled room and embraced me. "Oh my, oh my," he said huskily. "The risks you have taken this night. This night of nights." He released me from his sharp, uncomfortable embrace, stepped back two steps, and gazed fondly at me. "How proud, how very proud I am of you."

My lips quivered and, not knowing why, I found myself on the verge of tears. I found myself on the verge of tears with the jolt of surprise and horror felt by a blindfolded man who finally whisks off the playful kerchief and realizes himself to be on the edge of a precipice. And is it merely your imagination, or is every shimmering, windblown shrub begging you to plunge?

"You are my first success," Mr. Worthington said. "After all of these long hard years. My very first success."

Still breathing with some difficulty I said, "You mean I'm the first one who's gotten caught?"

"First one caught?" Mr. W. asked with a light chuckle. "Paul, you're the first one to even *try* to leave." He shook his head.

I felt I could be frank with Worthington. "Are you going to kill me?" I asked.

"No," he said, "what ever gave you that idea?"

"Are you going to perform experiments on me?"

He laughed. He clasped his old hands together, threw back his head, and laughed almost soundlessly.

"You are, then?"

"No, no," he said, looking at me again and smiling. "Not at all. In fact, in a few moments I am going to conditionally release you from your contract here. I suspect that my confidence in you is premature, perhaps even misplaced, but you have taken extraordinary risks and you deserve, I believe, another crack at things on the outside. Oh, I will be criticized, of that I am more than certain. We believe that those who come here deserve fully to stay here. But when NESTER was set up in the beginning of this century — it was not called NESTER then, for acronyms were neither popular nor common — but when this organization was first set up we said that rehabilitation was one of our prime objectives. Yet we have rehabilitated no one. Our only service has been to occupy our clients, to give them every opportunity to live out their destructive desires, and our sole comfort is in the fact that they are harming no one, that their so-called administrative abilities and scientific insights go no further than the orbit we have allowed them." He stopped, took another step back, and looked at me. "But there I go," he said. "Rambling on like this. By the look of you, I'm quite quite sure you haven't the vaguest idea what I am talking about. Do you?"

I shook my head. I felt limp.

"Well, there's still a little time. I want to get you out of here. I've already reported to *my* superiors" — he glanced upward — "that I am releasing you from the compound, and I want to make that a fact before someone decides to contradict me. I'm not going to have this success taken from me."

"You mean I'm going back to my old life?"

171

"I mean no such thing. Don't even mention that. Put it completely out of mind. Your old life ended when you answered our advertisement. It is gone forever. And I'm afraid I have nothing particularly enticing to offer you in its place. But whatever you do or wherever you go, you will at least be out of here. I swear to you, Paul, I'll never understand why more of you boys don't bolt. We do everything to encourage you to hightail it out of here, but you're my very first chicken to fly the coop. Oh goodness, I keep saying that. I'm still beside myself. Well, come on. My car's waiting below."

We took an elevator down past the ground floor into the basement. The doors glided open and we got off in the data-processing chamber. The giant computer was still whirring away but there was only a skeleton crew minding it, pacing around the enormous instrument, holding clipboards and jotting notes, playing hasty arpeggios on handy key punch machines. Mr. Worthington and I were unnoticed. We walked through narrow aisles, past empty desks separated by frosted glass partitions, until we came to a heavy metal door guarded by an old man in a lime green uniform, exactly like the one worn by Mr. Acoraci.

"Good evening, Mr. Kilke," Mr. Worthington said to the elderly guard.

"Good evening, Mr. Worthington," said the old man with a smile.

"I'll be out for perhaps an hour, Mr. Kilke."

"Very well, sir," said the old man, rising. He shuffled over to the heavy metal door and pulled it open with some effort. Beyond the door was a long black limousine. The sleek car's motor was idling, and its expensive purr echoed subtly on the smooth concrete walls that surrounded it.

172

"Oh good, my car is here," said Mr. W. He took me by the arm and led me to it. The windows were draped in light gray curtains. In the front seat sat a uniformed driver with a young, tan face and perfect, expressionless features. His blond hair curled out from beneath his black chauffeur's cap.

I got into the car and it began to move almost undetectably up the concrete ramp. "You've had quite a night," said Mr. Worthington, patting my arm.

Soft music filled the car. Strange, compelling music made by vibraphones, flutes, and drums that beat as gently as tiny bird hearts. I breathed deeply. A scent of flowers. "Where are you taking me?" I asked.

The car emerged from the uphill runway and we were in the NESTER parking lot. A light rain was falling and the headlights stabbed into the thickening night. "Let me ask *you* a question," said Mr. Worthington. "Where were you going? Be honest."

We moved onto the highway. "I was going to Boston."

"Why?"

There was no reason to mince words. "To expose you."

"Me?" he asked, touching his chest with one finger.

"You, yes. Not you personally. The whole thing. The organization. The whole thing. The illegal experiments. The kidnapings. The electronic implantations. The marketing surveys. The thugs, the madmen . . ." I was getting a little worked up again, though I was very fatigued. I sat up straighter, hoping to revive myself a little. "I was going to call a press conference and alert everyone."

"Oh please," said Mr. W. "Don't talk like that. If any of my superiors were to hear that they'd seriously question my wisdom in releasing you from your contract. It reminds one so clearly of your original fantasies, the ones with which you came to us. The fame, the grandeur. It is all the same thing. These desires to be in the newspapers, to testify, to be a celebrity." He carefully placed a Lifesaver in his mouth, sucked on it for a moment, and then shook his head. "So the less said about that, the better."

"Where are you taking me?" I asked.

"I am taking you to Boston. We will say good-bye, Paul. I am, you see, quite determined that you shall be treated as our first rehabilitated recruit. Your period with us, I feel, has been a remarkable one. When you were first brought to NESTER you were a frustrated and angry man whose spiritual malignancy allowed him to agree — not to say desire — to do all varieties of unforgivable experiments. You were, in short, a dangerous man.

"You see, Paul, that is what we do. We collect men such as yourself and keep them away from others so they will do no harm. The experiments are fake. The films are fake. The intercepted letters, the EEGs, the GSRs— all fabrications. You, quite understandably, I suppose, never became aware of that. But you *did* feel an admirable revulsion with your work, and, believe me, that is rare. Moreover, you were willing to act on your revulsion and that, Paul, has until this night been unheard of. None of the people who visit us ever ever leave. They never wake up from their dreams. It is deeply sad. But, of course, we can only be happy that at least they are with us, where they can do no harm. Yet we give them every chance to leave. We tempt them at every turn."

174

"Every chance to leave?" I said, shaking my head and trying to keep up with him. "Then why the spying, why the guards, why the terror and strict enforcement of rules?"

"Three reasons. First, our clients like it. It amuses, titillates them, and fulfills fantasies that humane conditions never would. Second, it gives work to our nonscientific recruits. Many of our clients are only thugs, lonely men who would, if we did not stop them, join secret police organizations or become soldiers of fortune; others would be, say, tyrannical office managers. We take care of all sorts. And the third reason is that, while our people are with us, we must punish them. We must work them, discipline them, scold them, frighten them, and make them hop. Their nasty little dreams must come true with a vengeance. Charity, Paul, must have its sterner side. The individuals who founded NESTER believed in punishment."

"You make it sound like an act of God," I said with a small, frightened sneer.

"I firmly believe," he answered, "that the will of God is present in everything we do."

"What's going to happen to me?"

"I imagine you would like me to say that it is entirely up to you. But that, sadly, is not the case." He reached beneath the soft beige seat and produced a wallet. Here is a wallet with a generous sum of money and cards with which you can establish a new identity. You will become the person whose name appears on the cards. You will receive, for one year, a monthly check. You will not lead a life entirely open to all options. You will not, for in-

175

stance, live on the east coast. You will not reestablish contact with old friends or family. You will not teach. You will not engage in any scientific activities. And you must start from the beginning, an unknown man, no longer young. We have no halfway houses. You are, as I've said, our first rehabilitee."

We entered the city limits, and lights from signs and stores we passed slipped across Mr. Worthington's face. He leaned forward and tapped on the glass that separated us from the driver. "Jeremiah," he said, "please proceed to Boston City Hospital and stop there."

"Why are you taking me there?" I asked.

He ignored my question. "I only hope that you are truly ready to be on your own. I know the old desires are still within you, like the end of a splinter improperly removed. Yet you have come a long way and I am willing to take a chance on you. Our facilities are limited. We cannot incarcerate every foolish man and woman who wishes to violate the sanctity of the human mind. We have only four installations, aside from this one outside of Boston, and each one can only handle a couple of hundred. Usually we have to wait until a death before we can gather someone new in. And there are so many who rightfully belong with us. This city alone is filled with all kinds of minor-league mind robbers — advertising men, disc jockeys, private detectives — not to mention the mind robbers of the first rank who call this city home. But we can only do so much. Our resources and time are limited." He smiled at me. "If only our people responded to our environment as you did, then we could really do some good. But we have no turnover. The people we take stay with us for the rest of their lives. Our only break is an occasional suicide. And that's not very satisfying, is it?"

"No sir," I said. The rain was falling harder now, splashing onto the car's long, dark hood and beating soundlessly against the windows.

"Well, our time together is almost up, Paul. I am looking forward to sleep. I'm so tired."

"I'm tired, too."

"I can well imagine." The car glided to a stop. "We are at the hospital."

"I don't understand," I insisted.

"I am going to let you out and you will check into this hospital. You have a Blue Cross card and you will be admitted."

"Why am I going to the hospital?"

Again, he reached beneath the seat. This time he came up with an enormous knife with a black wooden handle. "And so it is good-bye," he said.

"Good-bye, sir," I said, looking at him and feeling for the door handle. I edged away.

"There *is* one more thing before we part. You see, I am aware that your dissatisfaction with us was not the product of the most noble and humane feelings. Your disaffection was, to say the least, complicated. And some of your unhappiness was, I think, for frankly reprehensible reasons. But you acted, you fought, and that is what we are willing to concentrate on, for now. You are rewarded."

"Thank you, sir," I said, lunging for the door. It was locked.

He moved closer to me. He rested his hand on my shoulder. "But you cannot altogether escape your punishment.

177

I think that would be too much to expect and I don't think such utter leniency would do you much good. However, I am completely confident that you will consider this far better —"

"Oh no, sir," I said trying the door again. I tried to stand up and I hit my head against the car's ceiling. I slumped to the seat.

"— you will consider this far better than your previous punishment. You will remember always to be careful." I tried to squirm from his grip and he held me tighter. Then reaching over quickly with the knife in his hand, he cut off my hand in one smooth, easy motion.

He put me out in front of the hospital and then he and his chauffeur drove away. Numb, I made a few steps in the direction of the receding car. The back lights were dark red. The rain was falling with some insistence. My mind was shaking with a thousand questions. I wanted to call out to him. Then I glanced at my bloody wrist and perhaps the pain was awakened by the visual reinforcement, I don't know. But instead of asking any questions or calling any names I began to scream and that seemed enough — occupying, as it did, more of my brain, my heart, and my soul than anything had in quite some time.